Skinner's Cay

Ann Orsini

The contents of this work, including, but not limited to, the accuracy of events, people, and places depicted; opinions expressed; permission to use previously published materials included; and any advice given or actions advocated are solely the responsibility of the author, who assumes all liability for said work and indemnifies the publisher against any claims stemming from publication of the work.

All Rights Reserved
Copyright © 2019 by Ann Orsini

No part of this book may be reproduced or transmitted, downloaded, distributed, reverse engineered, or stored in or introduced into any information storage and retrieval system, in any form or by any means, including photocopying and recording, whether electronic or mechanical, now known or hereinafter invented without permission in writing from the publisher.

Dorrance Publishing Co
585 Alpha Drive
Suite 103
Pittsburgh, PA 15238
Visit our website at *www.dorrancebookstore.com*

ISBN: 978-1-4809-5456-4
eISBN: 978-1-4809-5431-1

Dedication

This book is dedicated to my mother, Ann Mattera, who always accepted people for who they were and lived each and every day as if she was on an exotic vacation. Life was her paradise!

Introduction

May 5th, 2011, 10:00 a.m.

"Mom."

"Asterid?"

"Mom."

I could hear those voices in my sleep. They were the voices of my husband and my boys calling me from the bottom of the stairs. Now I was awake thanks to them, but I did not mind. They were the best part of every day. Speaking of the day, it was a sunny one because the sun was shining through the skylight in my bedroom like a warm welcoming from Mother Nature to begin my day, that and the continuous yelling coming up the stairs.

"I'm up," I said. "I will be right down."

But it was too late, my husband was on his way up asking me, "Honey, where is the new train set you bought for the boys? Your father is going to set it up for them at his place so they can play with it today while they are over there."

I said, "I think I put it in the closet over there," as I pointed to the bedroom closet. *Where things entered only to disappear,* I thought. Then I went over and opened the door and said, "I will find it, don't worry." I started to rummage through the shelves and right before my eyes, there it was. "Here it is, "I said.

"The train set?" my husband asked.

"No. I'll find the train set," I said as I continued to search.

Then he walked over to help me search and said, "Ohhhh, that's what you found. Your journal."

He took it off the shelf and continued to harass me saying, "The infamous Skinner's Cay, your vacation in paradise. You could have ended up there with that crazy man and his crazy brothers."

"Stop it," I said. "You know I love you."

He started to laugh and said, "Then you won't mind if I read it or are you having second thoughts about me?"

"No, I love you but I have not even read it since I wrote it." I kept looking in the closet as I spoke and there was the box with the train set. "Here is the train," I said

He picked it up because it was big and heavy.

"I don't know how I could lose it," I said.

"Okay, I'm taking the boys to your dad's and when I come back, I'll read your journal," he said.

"Maybe you will," I said.

He laughed and went on his way mumbling, "Sexy nightgown!"

I laughed because it was sexy, white, long, and see-through which is why I needed to find my bathrobe. *I could not walk around the house like this*, I thought as I took the green journal with big black writing on it that read "Skinner's Cay". I went over to the bed, sat down, and stared at the book.

It seemed like such a long time ago, I thought as I opened the journal and began to read...

Day One – May 1, 2005

I turned to wave one final good-bye to my father at the airport. I would soon be departing for a long overdue vacation to the Bahamas and felt overwhelmed with the anticipation of it all. I had never had a real vacation, not one to speak of at least, and my demanding career had consumed me. Though rewarding, being a clinical psychologist was draining, so it was time.

In a few hours I was to arrive in Nassau and board the ferry to 'paradise', as it is called. "Would you care for some caviar and champagne?" the airline stewardess asked.

At that moment I thought, *Yes! First class*. Then I answered, "Yes, thank you."

I'd planned this vacation carefully, contemplating quite a few travel destinations before deciding to choose this one, Skinner's Cay.

Skinner's Cay was an exclusive vacation resort owned by a family of five brothers and open only certain months of the year. Reservations are made up to five years in advance, because of the resort's fine reputation and the high demand of certain types of tourists. The resort was private, secluded, and quite pricey. There is even an application required before being accepted as a guest. It sounds strange, But in reading about the island, the Skinners pride themselves in being able to accommodate each guest in a special way.

A window seat alone in First Class with caviar and champagne, what could be more serene?

Then the pilot announced, "Good morning, ladies and gentlemen, we will be arriving at our destination as scheduled in one hour and fifty minutes."

Butterflies consumed my stomach as I realized that this was really it! I would soon embark on a seven-day tour of paradise: a journey of sun, sand and beach. Swimming in the Atlantic, eating lobster, and just doing nothing if I chose to.

I was a little sad though, my dad declined my invitation to join me and, being that my mom passed two years ago, she could not join me. So here I am, me, myself, and I, on the trip of a lifetime. Mom would have been so excited. I'm sure she is.

"Welcome to the Bahamas," I heard the pilot announce.

That was fast, I thought. My daydreams must have consumed me most of the flight and now here I was. I scurried about to get off the plane and headed straight for the taxi terminal. It did not take long for me to find my driver, a tall dark man with dark hair, brown eyes, and a slender build. He was dressed comfortably in khakis, a cotton shirt, and sandals. He was standing in the airport lobby holding a huge sign that read, "Welcome Miss Asterid!" He had a sun-worn face and a big smile. As I walked toward him, he could tell it was me.

"Hello," I said, "I am Asterid."

"Hello, Miss Asterid. I am Bahmi. Welcome to Nassau, I will be driving you to your water taxi launch." His accent and appearance assured me I was in good hands, a true islander.

"Thank you," I said. "But my luggage?"

"No worries! It's already in taxi!"

Ok then, I thought and followed Bahmi outside where I stepped into a different world, a world of sunshine and a warming and delightful energy of good.

He opened the door to the taxi and welcomed me once again as he closed my door. Still inspired by my surroundings, I gazed out the window as we commenced to the ferry or, as he called it, water taxi.

He smiled in the rear-view mirror and said, "So you are vacationing at Skinner's Cay. Correct?"

"Yes," I said.

Before I could say any more, he spoke. "Lucky girl, I hear it is a most wonderful paradise."

"I know! I heard that too. I'm very excited about it," I said.

Soon he pulled over and stopped the vehicle.

"Well, here we are, your destination." He jumped out of the taxi and ran around to open my door. I got out.

"Thank you," I said.

"Most welcome, Miss!"

He seemed more eager than I did. *I hope all the islanders are as jolly as he!*

Bahmi unloaded my luggage from the trunk and wheeled it down a long dock in the middle of a huge ocean.

When we reached the water taxi, I knew why it wasn't called a ferry. It was not very big and had two rows of five seats each, but looked very comfortable.

The captain got up from his seat and greeted us, "Bahmi, Miss Asterid, welcome. I am Captain."

Well, I certainly will remember his title, easy enough. I smiled and replied, "Hello, Captain."

He was not too tall and not too thin, but pleasant looking. He sounded like me so I assumed he was from the U.S.. Before I could utter another word, he took my luggage from Bahmi and placed all five suitcases on the floor of the boat. Bahmi shook his hand, gave me a hug, and strolled back up the dock, waving goodbye about five times.

"Bye, thank you!" I exclaimed.

Captain took my hand while I stepped into the boat and told me, "Pick a seat, anyone you want. You are the only passenger."

"Ok then, I shall." I sat on the lawn chair-type seat with a white cushion. The boat was blue, small but pleasant.

Captain, dressed in whites with boat shoes and a captain's hat, proceeded to the captain's chair and took the wheel. "Off to paradise!" he shouted. "Shall we depart, Miss?"

"Yes, if I am the only passenger."

"You are indeed." He started the engine and took off and not slowly either!

Captain was pleasant enough and there was plenty of room on the boat, even with my five large suitcases consuming the most space. Yes, I did not skimp at all. My five Victoria's Secret "Pink" suitcases were well stocked with dresses, skirts, blouses, shorts, capris, yoga wear, bathing suits, lingerie, makeup, accessories, and bath needs. All from Victoria's Secret of course, you could say I'm obsessed. I did splurge this time because I figured if I'm taking such an extravagant vacation, $10,000 dollars a night to elaborate, then I may as well go all the way and I did! I needed this, work and my mom's illness have taken a toll on me and it was time for some relaxing.

"So Miss Asterid, why Skinner's Cay? Anyone you know that has been?"

"No, I did plenty of research on vacation destinations and this seemed to be perfect. Why do you ask? Ever been?"

"Yes, every seven days I make the trip ten times," and he laughed.

I laughed too, though I thought he was mistaken, "What about the guests returning from the island?

And with that thought he added, "I do not bring guests returning from the island, there is a separate water taxi for that. There you go," he said, answering my question without even asking.

I would certainly call that service. The fact that I am the only guest on the water taxi, I just had to provoke him, "So you mean to say that each guest gets their own private trip to the island in your taxi?"

"No Miss, each group, usually two traveling together. But yes, single guests travel separately. It gives one that personalized attention and keeps the travel organized."

"So how long have you been a captain?" I asked.

"Oh, about fifteen years. Since I was sixteen."

"That would make you thirty-one."

"Yes, it would. I look good for my age is what you are thinking. Correct?"

He laughed once more. I could not tell if he was serious, but I was thinking he was in his forties.

"I am from your part of the states, Massachusetts. You are Rhode Island, yes?"

"Yes," I said. "Providence, Rhode Island. What brings you to Nassau?"

"What wouldn't?" he said. "The sun, the sand, the ocean, and the vacation. I like the atmosphere all year round!"

"I can't argue," I assured him.

"Actually," he continued, "My parents bought property here years ago cheap. They loved vacationing here so much they decided to make it our home, so here we are. The water taxi business was my father's idea, but I do most of the trips so Mom and Dad can feel like they are on a permanent vacation."

"How sweet," I said. "That is so generous."

"Well, they are great people and have been good parents. I just wanted to give back a little."

I took my phone from my handbag to look at the time and captain immediately intervened, "You won't get cell phone reception here, nor anywhere else from here on in."

"Just checking the time," I said.

"It's one o'clock."

I looked down at my phone and he was right.

"I just check the position of the sun. That's a one o'clock sun if I do say so!" he exclaimed.

"You're good," I added.

"Yes, ma'am. No clocks on this ship."

Ok, I thought. *This is not a ship, but he was exactly on the time and I knew I would have no reception once we departed, which was fine by me. I wanted the entire feel of being apart from the rest of the world*. Captain just kept thrashing through the waves and I was inhaling my surroundings. The warm air and sun consumed me and the ocean seemed to consume the entire island like turquoise crystals in a large swimming pool.

"How long is this trip?" I asked the captain.

He turned to me, light brown hair blowing across his sunburned face and greenish gray eyes peeking through all beneath his hat. "About two hours," then he slowed the boat, got up, and went over to this big metal box next to his seat, "Time for a drink."

"You are not drinking now, are you?"

He laughed once more, took out two bottles of water, and handed one to me. I smiled and took the refreshment. "Thank you, I am so thirsty."

"We have chips if you want," he offered.

"No, water is fine."

He sat and began steering, "Here we go." He merrily drove and I chugged my water like a dehydrated fish.

Wow that sun is hot after a while in it.

Captain's hair wasn't the only thing out of control, mine was blowing like a red flag in the air and across my face. I took my scrunchie from my tiny wrist and put my hair in a makeshift bun. That was better. I was actually starting to cool down. Now I could relax and enjoy the ride, maybe I would see some big fish like whales or dolphins, that would be inspiring!

But the mind does not rest, or at least mine didn't, so there I was again bothering captain, "So how many trips to the island have you made today?"

He said, "Yours' is the fourth, one more after you and I'm finished for the day. Don't worry Miss, there will be other people there. You are not being kidnapped."

I guess he could sense my insecurities. Not that I would mind being the only guest, I'm all for R and R, I just have never had such a personalized vacay before. *I'll just take a nap*, I thought.

But that did not work, so I took out my journal and inside I had an itinerary tucked between the pages. A plan of my entire week, so far I was on schedule. I planned to arrive at the island before five, get acquainted with my resort, and had an entire outfit picked out for dinner. It was so exciting to be able to dress for an occasion other than work. Suits and briefcases were what I was accustomed to, not sundresses and lounge-around attire. As for my journal, I will complete each day with an entry. I do not want any moment to escape my thoughts, even after I return home.

"How are you doing back there?" asked Captain.

"Fine, gorgeous view." Just then a huge wave came over the sides of the boat. Not big enough to make an impact, but enough to get a significant spray of humidity.

How delightful it felt on my hot face, a hat would have been a good idea but I'm a sun sucker, can't get enough.

"How are you, Captain? You must be tired, navigating all day."

"No, I love the sea and its magic."

"Good enough," I said. "Glad you are enjoying yourself."

"We'll be there soon Miss, don't worry."

"Oh, I'm enjoying myself already, I'm not worried." I closed my eyes to rest them. I must have dozed for quite some time, because before I knew it we were approaching land.

A sun-gleamed landscape of waving coconut palms and dancing flowers of purple, yellow, and orange awaited as the boat launched.

I looked to captain and said, "How long did I sleep? It's beautiful, isn't it?"

"A few hours, and yes indeed it is beautiful. Paradise to its fullest, wouldn't you say Miss?" he said.

Captain took my hand and escorted me off the boat, onto the dock, and then he turned to gather my luggage. Without missing a beat, a man appeared with a dolly for the luggage. A beautiful man with blue eyes, shoulder-length blonde hair, and a physique of a gym master.

He smiled, shook my hand and said, "Hello Miss Asterid, I am Jonas, your host. Welcome to Skinner's Cay."

Mystified by my surroundings and obviously awe stricken, I answered him abruptly, "Hello, happy to meet you. Thank you for having me."

Then he turned to Captain. They hugged, probably for the tenth time today, and Jonas helped Captain transfer my luggage from the boat to the dolly as if they were handling rare jewels.

I also gave Captain a hug, he seemed like the huggy type and why not, it was such an exhilarating atmosphere for everyone. Tipping was not allowed, they were included in the vacation package. It was an all-inclusive ten thousand dollars a day, *that's fair I guess.*

Jonas pulled the dolly and nodded his head, "Shall we begin?"

"Yes of course," I said following him down the dock, which took us to a long stretch of crystal-like beach sand. The kind you like to sink your feet in like a plush new carpet, so soothing and fun. I didn't mind if I did, sink my feet that is, so I indulged. I took off my gold flip flops and kneaded the glorious sand, my turquoise sarong skirt blowing in the breeze, my long red hair waving about again, scrunchie on my wrist. I go back and forth all day, hair up, then down, and so on. It's a habit I guess.

Jonas laughed as I played in the sand. I giggled childishly as we continued toward a big bright yellow vehicle. *A dune buggy!* I thought, *how appropriate.*

To the occasion, traveling the island paradise in an adult version of the Barbie beach buggy I had when I was a kid.

Jonas assisted me as I climbed up into the vehicle, loaded my luggage into the back, and hopped into the driver's side. "Shall we proceed?" he asked.

"Yes, yes, yes!" I exclaimed.

We traveled a long, narrow path smothered with scenery. Myriad flowing palms and waving colorful flowers dancing on white sand, contrasted by the aquamarine-blue sea. All consumed by the tropical ocean breeze, as if all was a tribute to me.

"We will be there in a few minutes," Jonas said.

"Oh good," I said. But I was quite content with just riding and absorbing the enchanting atmosphere. How delighted I was already!

"Here we are," he announced. "This is our lovely resort." It was lovely indeed! "Miss Asterid, our home will be your home for the next seven days. May I add, you have certainly planned appropriately. May is the finest month here on the island. The weather is perfect, usually 85 degrees, and the ocean is calm, especially for swimming. You do like to swim?" He smiled, nodding and waited for my answer.

"Oh yes," I said. "My mother taught me when I was very young. She loved to swim too, people used to call her Esther Williams."

He laughed. I was unsure if that meant he knew who Esther Williams was or if he did not. Then he said, "Esther Williams. Great swimmer. So, you do know of her?"

"Yes I do, but my brother Lucas is the great swimmer of the family. He is like a fish."

Just then a tall slender man with dark hair, dark eyes, and a straw hat came up to the vehicle. "Hello," he excitedly greeted us.

"This is Tevin Jonas. Tevin, this is Miss Asterid."

"Hello," I said and he helped me out of the buggy, "Thank you."

I no sooner started toward the back of the buggy to claim my luggage. He was already loading it onto a cart, sort of like a golf cart.

Jonas continued, "Tevin will escort your luggage to your chalet if you would like a refreshment here at our tiki bar."

And what a tiki bar! It was a big square bar with straw like stools and occupied a corner of the beach area. On the left was a big chalet style structure, almost like a house, and as I looked in amazement, Jonas stated, "That is the dining hut, attached is the main desk."

Before I could ask, he noticed me looking behind all of that to a huge pointed chalet bigger than the dining hut. It was set way back, but one couldn't help but see the roof peaking up to eternity.

"My brothers and I live there in case you were wondering."

"Yes," I said. "It's so big," I added.

"Well, there are four of us."

"How nice," I said, "and yes I'll have that refreshment."

"Pina colada coming up," the man at the bar shouted. He came running over to me with a glorious glass of cheer with an umbrella, straw, cherries, and pineapples decorating my glass.

I sipped quite vigorously then I laughed and muttered, "Thirsty." It tasted so good and so refreshing because by this time the sun was gleaming.

Jake was standing there. "Welcome Miss Asterid, glad to have you here."

"Oh, thank you Jake. I am so delighted and everyone has been so courteous to me."

Jake was medium height, medium build, about fifty years old, and I could recognize his accent. It was different than that of Tevin and Bahmi, so not quite from the Bahamas.

I asked, "Where are you from, Jake?"

"Oh yes," he chuckled. "I don't quite sound the same as Tevin, right?"

I nodded and said, "I'm not being rude. Am I?"

"No ma'am, not a bit rude. I am from South Africa, but I lived in Hawaii for thirty years and now I live here on Skinner's Cay."

"Wow you have made the rounds, haven't you?" I said.

"Yes ma'am, I am delighted to have ended up here in such a paradise!"

It was such a perfect day. I felt catered to already and I had only been there an hour or so. It was as if I was the only guest. Maybe I was, but I hoped not. That would have been weird.

But it was agonizing me, so I had to ask, "Where are the other guests Jake?"

"Oh, they are all here, You are the last to arrive, they are settling in their chalets and relaxing before dinner."

Well that's a relief, I thought, *not that I mind my privacy but all these people catering to just me would have been too much.* Tevin must have taken off to drop my bags off. I did not notice him leave and the pina colada was occupying my attention. It was very strong, but very satisfying indeed.

Jonas had disappeared too, I think he stepped into the office. It was just me and Jake. I edged my way over to a barstool to get out of the constant beaming sun. Jake busied himself rearranging bottles and glasses while dodging hanging plants and flowers which hung from the roof of the tiki bar. I was soon feeling relaxed enough to unwind, when before I knew it Tevin was back.

"Miss Asterid, would you like to commence to your chalet? You can see it from here," he said as he pointed to a most adorable structure with purple shutters.

I thought, *Purple?* The questionnaire asked my favorite color. What a coincidence, or not. Well anyway, how splendid!

"Oh thanks Tevin, but if it is all the same to you I'll walk when I finish my drink."

He took off in his buggy humming a tune and smiling.

Jake then spoke, "I do not blame you. My drinks are so enticing, are they not?"

"Yes they are Jake, very delicious and satisfying! But I must head to my chalet. I hear the dinners here are most enticing as well."

"That they are Miss, that they are. You go now and we will see you tonight at eight."

"Yes, you will and thanks again for the refreshing refreshment, Jake."

He nodded with a smile and I began towards my quarters.

My chalet was the first one on the island, only about an eighth of a mile from the main beach area. *How convenient,* I thought. I walked down a long dock to my chalet which was totally surrounded by the ocean. The only means to land was the dock or a boat. *How extravagant*, I thought. *My own little house on the ocean...literally*! The structure was made of palm, like a straw house. It even looked like it was woven. It had little windows, one on each side and two doors, one on the dock side and one on the front deck side facing the ocean. It was marvelous and I had not even gone in yet.

Inside was better than I imagined. It was like walking into an extravagant dollhouse only better because this place was not cold and lifeless, but warm and cozy. I felt as if I was the doll, this place was made for me. The kitchenette and sitting room were a lovely, combined open space. The kitchen area hosted a quaint round white table made of rattan with two cute chairs to match. On it stood a handmade basket of fresh fruit, seagrapes, coconut slices, brown fruit, and hibiscus flowers. These are sweet and edible and grow copiously on the island.

Next to the sink, which was set right under one of the windows that overlooked the ocean, was a counter stocked with a coffee maker, packets of Dunkin Donuts coffee, creamers, and sugar. Next to this display was a basket of imported cheeses, crackers, and champagne. There was a small Frigidaire in the corner and it was filled with bottled water, sparkling water, wines, and more champagne.

I walked across the whitewashed wooden floor to the sitting area, a large white sofa, smothered with seashell shaped throw pillows of many colors like aqua, coral lilac and yellow. It was so inviting, I had to plop down to try it out and it was as pleasurable to sit on as it looked. The end table next to where I sat held a basket of fresh flowers, not edible, but a collage of colors, yellow, pink, purple, orange. They were beautiful and smelled heavenly too!

I could have stayed on the sofa for the rest of the evening. It was so comfortable, so relaxing. Then I noticed the room off to the side, it was separated by a doorway of hanging strands of ivory seashells made like a curtain. I walked through to a room with a large canopy bed, sheer purple drapes flowed from the canopy and it had a white eyelet bedspread. I'm sure my favorite colors of purple and white reappearing over and over wasn't a coincidence. I was delighted. The bedroom had a cute little vanity, white rattan of course with a mirror. There was a dresser against the wall and a separate wardrobe in the corner for my garments.

Most interesting of all, in the far corner was another little doorway leading to the bathroom which consisted of all the amenities one would expect except for the tub, a giant seashell. Yes, that's what it was. A big shell I could swim in if I chose. It was aqua like the ocean and had jets like a jacuzzi, to make waves I suppose, and a stand attached with a showerhead. Also a bar that circled the top with a wrap-around curtain. A basket of soaps, lotions, and shampoos were set on a little vanity near the sink. I knew I would be quite comfortable here for the duration of my stay.

It seemed all my likings were at my disposal. The questionnaire, that must have been the reason. When I filled out the application for this vacation, it included a book of questions about my likes and dislikes. Now I know why Skinner's Cay aims to please. *I should be unpacking about now, but I really need a nice shower*, I thought.

Suddenly something was beeping throughout the chalet! I ran to the other room to see what it was, and there I saw it, an intercom on the wall near the sofa. I believed someone was trying to contact me. I pressed the button which read "speak".

"Hello, this is Asterid," I waited.

"Yes," a voice proclaimed. "How are we doing Miss?"

"Who is there?" I asked.

"Hello Miss Asterid. It's Tevin. I will be driving you to dinner up at the dining chalet."

"Oh, I wasn't expecting a call. I thought there were no phones or reception on the island."

"Ha ha ha," he laughed strangely or maybe normally for him. "Just intercoms," he added.

"Ok," I said. "What time is dinner, Tevin?"

"Eight o'clock, Miss. I will be there in about an hour."

An hour, I thought! "What time is it now?"

"Six forty-five, Miss. Is six forty-five fine for you?"

"It is, but I would like to walk. Is that fine, Tevin?"

"It is, Miss. Except I am assigned to you for the duration of your stay. I am here for whatever you wish."

"Thank you Tevin," I said graciously. "But we have the next week for you to assist me. I really would enjoy the walk it is so close to my chalet. See you soon!"

I really needed to start getting ready for dinner but I had not explored the deck yet. It was located right off the kitchen area. So I ventured through the doorway to a porch of incredible ocean waves, crashing magnificently against the deck. There was a wicker lounger with big purple cushions. *The questionnaire again,* I thought. *My colors were purple and white, they seemed to have me pegged.*

I longed just to take in the tropical breeze, but time was passing and I was no closer to being ready for dining than I was an hour ago. I discovered an outdoor shower at the edge of the deck. It was semi closed in and had three sides with the doorway open, facing the ocean. It too made of plain wood. I danced over to it, pulling off my clothes, and danced under a shower of exhilarating warm water. It even had a shelf of shower gels, shampoos, and whatever other toiletries I could ever need.

I lathered my five-foot, ninety-pound, tan body with passion fruit body wash, inhaling the warm tropical air, exhaling breaths of serenity. I was naked to the sun and the entity of marine life swimming graciously in the large body of water in front of my deck. I washed my long red hair, some would say strawberry blonde, with the shampoo that smelled like wild berries. It was refreshing! That's I how I felt, refreshed. I could have stayed in the shower all night, but time was ticking and my stomach was rumbling. I had not eaten since the caviar on the plane, I was starving actually.

I grabbed a towel off the rack of the shower, dried off quickly, and wrapped it around my head. I ran to my suitcase marked "dresses" and took out my Victoria's Secret aquamarine lace maxi dress.

Then I went to the suitcase marked "lingerie" and took out my gel bra, I needed all the help I could get in that department. Along with a pair of matching panties, lace of course and the same color as my dress. It was just a bit OCD. I dressed eagerly in front of a dresser in the bedroom so I could see how I looked at the same time. *I look beautiful,* I thought. I had to think that because I was always so critical of myself. If I started nit-picking, I would not go to dinner at all. "Positive thoughts," that's what I say to my patients. Ironic, right?

Looking in the mirror, I noticed my face was burned from the sun all day. So just a shimmer lotion would do and a bit of lip gloss, clear but shiny gloss. I towel-dried my hair because I knew it would dry on the way to the dining hut, took my silver thong sandals from the shoe bag, and hurried to the dock. *Here goes*, I thought, *time to get acquainted*.

I strolled down the path, my dress flowing across my small but firm legs, feeling like the Little Mermaid en route to a Disney parade. The warm blow of wind caressed my sunburned cheeks, but continued to dry my long hair on the way. It was such an extraordinary feeling! A new place and a new adventure to call my own.

"Welcome Miss Asterid," a voice called, it was Jonas.

Or was it? There were four of them! All looked identical, all wore welcoming smiles, a white silk shirt, black pleated pants, and all were smiling at me with gleaming blue eyes and golden strands of blonde hair that stretched to shoulder length.

"Oh goodness," I said, "there are four of you."

"Five," said one of the men. "You have already met Jonas," he pointed to the brother on his right.

"I am Lucas, your activity director. Welcome."

The man on his left spoke next. "I am Rupert, your restauranteur," he exclaimed which made sense. The sign above the hut read, "Rupert's Seafood Fare."

"Enjoy," he said.

The last man in line said, "I am Sebastian, your entertainer. Welcome, miss."

Jonas added, "There is one more brother, he will not be joining us." Then silence, as if there was nothing more to speak of. Jonas interrupted the pause, "He is busy working on the other end of the island. Quenten is our accountant, book-keeper, and director. Behind the scenes, shall we say."

All nodded in agreement.

"Shall we proceed," he said and made a hand gesture as if he were courting me to walk the red carpet, as did his brothers.

"Well yes, thank you. It is a pleasure to meet all of you," I said as we continued into the dining area. "So, you are quintuplets."

"No," all chorused, "quadruplets."

"Quenten is our older brother," I don't know which one said it since by now they looked and sounded more and more alike.

The brothers then led me into an enormous room filled with light. It was bright, simple, but elegant. Loud but solemn, by this I mean the room was tiki torch lit. There were so many that the flames gave off a brightness flickering throughout the room. The light seemed to draw me in, it was like the dance floor of a disco, only toned down a lot. The room was simple, but designed to give off a feeling of elegance. This seemed to hypnotize me. So much so that the interruption by Jonas took me by surprise, I wasn't aware he was still behind me.

"Miss Asterid, to the left is the chef's area."

He pointed to a long table with glass in the front, for preparation I assumed, followed by three or four stainless steel stoves and ovens. There were fresh veggies and fruits in bins colorfully arranged like a collage of nutrition, huge boiling pots for lobsters, and cooks in the back working diligently to prepare our feast.

Then Jonas said, "Make yourself at home. Enjoy. I must join my brothers back out front, the other guests will be arriving."

There I was thinking I would be late and I was the first guest to arrive. *Oh I think I see champagne over on the back wall,* I thought. It was a big, clam shell shaped, ceramic champagne fountain made of crystal. It was sparkling, glistening and flowed with champagne right into little crystal glasses. I helped myself to one and sipped, maybe guzzled just a bit. It tasted so satisfying, my lips tingled with delight. I stood there by the fountain admiring the stucco white walls that were consumed by painted canvasses. Some were of the ocean, others were of palm trees and coconut trees.

One in particular consumed most of the wall on the right side of the hut. That one was a canvas of a man, a woman, and five boys in the room. I assumed it was a handsome young couple, the mom and dad, and five boys. The mom had long blonde hair and green eyes, the dad had short blonde hair and blue eyes, and all but one of the boys had shoulder length hair and blue eyes. The oldest son had a buzz cut and green eyes like a valley. This was a painting of the Skinner family when they were younger. I wondered where the parents were, not that it was my business.

The champagne was starting to kick in, so I had better stop wondering since that would lead to assuming things and my assumptions are never accurate. Still, I could not help but wonder why the oldest was not here to greet guests. I needed to stop. He was busy, the brothers said as much already. *Enough with this Asterid*, I said. *You are not a psychologist this week.*

Just as I surrendered to thinking, Jake the bartender entered with a roll away bar, a tiki bar on wheels. As he rolled over to a far corner, he waved. "Miss Matteo, how are you doing?"

"I'm good," I said as I raised my glass towards him and thought, *He even knows my last name. How charming!*

Jake had started to set up his glasses and bottles and lit little candles on the bar counter. He had a shaker and began shaking a concoction, pina coladas. He offered a glass to me.

"Oh yes, thanks." I took the drink as he took my empty glass. Just what I needed, more alcohol and no food. But it is vacation.

As I began to drink from my tall, frosted glass that was garnished with cherries, pineapple, and a colored decorative umbrella, I heard, "Miss Asterid! Miss Asterid!"

It was Jonas signaling to me to come to a big round table in the center of the room. I turned to Jake, smiled, and said, "Gotta go." Then he waved and smiled generously.

That was fast, I thought. In no time the white lace covered table was full, everyone was seated, and there was one empty chair, mine. So I hurried over to them and caught the aromas of our cuisine being prepared. I smelled grilled veggies and boiling lobsters.

I could not get my mind off the food at this point, so Jonas continued with his introduction, "Miss Asterid, the others are here."

"Oh, how nice," I said. "Hello," I said to all at the table.

They all smiled and Jonas continued, "This is Polly and Peggy, Dr. and Mrs. Reiner, Gregory and Colin Miranda, and Baby Emma."

"Nice to meet all of you," and I sat down. *Thank God*, I thought. Not that I wasn't happy to meet them, but I was getting dizzy from the two, no, three drinks, not counting the ones on the plane.

Polly and Peggy were beautiful twin girls with long blonde hair like strands of silk, blue eyes, and slender builds. They wore matching pastel sundresses, yellow with flowers, and white flip flops portraying a comfortable look. Dr. and Mrs. Reiner were an elderly, well-groomed, upper class couple in their seventies. She was a small woman with silver hair, green eyes, an abundance of makeup, probably Estee Lauder, and an expensive, peach, short sleeve maxi dress that I would guess was Gucci. The diamond on her finger that looked about five karats and it could light up a room. The doctor was a tall man with perfect posture, a medium build and salt and pepper hair. He too had green eyes. He wore tan dress slacks and a peach shirt that matched the lady.

Next were the newlyweds, as Jonas stated, Gregory and Georgio from Vermont. They were in their late twenties. Gregory was short and had a medium build, brown curly hair, brown eyes and wore a white polo shirt, khaki shorts, and tan loafers. Georgio was a tall, dirty blonde, hazel eyed, and somewhat shy man. He wore a tan t-shirt, stonewashed jeans, and flip flops. They seemed so happy together, glowing with excitement for life.

The final couple I was introduced to was quiet, conservative, and escorted what seemed to be a newborn. Colin, Miranda, and Baby Emma. Colin was of medium height and not quite medium build with strawberry blonde hair like mine. It was in a crew cut and he had hazel or brownish eyes. He wore a blue cotton shirt, khaki pants, and brown sandals. Miranda was naturally pretty with brown, shoulder length hair, and brown eyes. She had no makeup and olive skin that glowed. She was skinny with big boobs that I think she was trying to hide with a loose pink blouse. She wore a white maxi skirt and pink, flat ballerina-type slippers. Baby Emma, in a pink nightgown, was only concerned with her little white blanket. She was holding it while sitting in her carrier. She had a little brown fuzz on top of her head and had blue eyes, of course. They say all babies are born with blue eyes before they change to their permanent color.

While Jonas was finishing the introductions, Rupert politely interrupted him with a smile. "Dinner is being served, hope everyone has a hearty appetite."

On that note, all four brothers began wheeling carts over to the table. Perfectly portioned platters of seafood were placed in front of each guest. The silver platters contained an enormous lobster, I'd say five pounds at least, shrimp cocktail, conch salad, rice, peas, and a fruit bow.

"All of the foods are fresh from the sea and land of our island," Rupert exclaimed.

He was more excited than we were and I know I was very excited to finally see the feast. We all began consuming the succulent assortment and the brothers sat down with Jake, the bartender, in a corner of the room at a table they must have prepared for themselves while no one took notice. They too were feasting. *Well deserved*, I thought as warm drawn butter dripped down my lips after consuming a lobster claw, *mmmm delicious*.

Not all were inhaling the food like I was, some were taking their time sipping champagne in between little conversations with each other. But not me, my mouth was chewing continuously, no time for chatter. I laughed inside. As conversations grew, I learned that Polly and Peggy were on vacation as a graduation present from their parents. They had graduated from UCLA. Dr. and Mrs. Reiner were on their fifth trip to the island, they had been coming since it had opened. They were from New York City where the doctor had a practice for thirty years before retiring. Gregory and Georgio were on their honeymoon, I had assumed as much since they were introduced as newlyweds. They'd wed in Vermont a few days ago. Miranda needed to de-stress from childbirth, so Cole surprised her with a vacation, of course with the baby.

Then all at once there was silence and I think all eyes were on me. I took a sip of champagne to determine if I was correct and I knew by then it was. They were waiting for me to join in the conversation.

"So," I said, "I am here on my first real vacation, alone to enjoy myself."

Mrs. Reiner interrupted, "Where are you from dear?"

"Rhode Island," I said and all smiled acceptingly and continued to enjoy their meals. *That was easy*, I thought. I think they wanted me to be more of a participant than I was being, but I was just fine with my food and champagne. We had an entire week to become acquainted and I was not worried about "fitting in". I never was.

As the group continued laughing and eating, I started to look around. I felt as though I was being watched, though not by someone at the table this time nor anyone else in the room. A strange feeling came over me. It was the canvas, the painting of the Skinner family. It was the older brother, those blue green eyes were piercing through me or so it seemed. He was so mysterious, so life like, as if he wanted to speak. He was gorgeous, or at least in the painting he was, and why was he not here, it's his island too. He could have greeted us all and then gone back to finish his work. *Well, none of my business*, I thought and tried not to stare at him.

By now, platters were bare and my taste buds were gleaming with satisfaction. The atmosphere was absorbing and the brothers glowed with happiness for our approval of the feast. Jonas rose from his spot in the corner and approached our table. He made a gesture with his hand that suggest that we continue this celebration out on the back patio. The group followed the brothers outside a back door and onto a patio.

Sebastian then announced, "Now music and dancing, my guests."

The patio consisted of an area of South Beach white furniture, white sofas, chairs, and glass tables that supported small votive candles of gold flames, flickering to an ambience of melancholy.

A small stage to the left of the patio held a chair, a spotlight, and a microphone on a stand in front of the chair. Sebastian spoke again, inviting all to have a seat and get comfortable, so each guest did just that. All sat, drink in hand, and got ready for Sebastian as he took the stage with his guitar. The other brothers went back inside quietly, I assumed to help clean up. They had kitchen help, but it seemed that they performed most of the tasks themselves. They were very involved. I was still standing, stretching my legs a bit, and observing the young lovers, hopeful twins, and even the older lovers. Yes, just observing their togetherness by myself in this romantic, enticing setting. Then I remembered, I chose to travel alone. It was my gift to me and I was free to spend my days as I liked. This was an advantage, no one to answer to or please.

Sebastian started strumming his guitar and singing Jimmy Buffet's Margaritaville. He was very good. Soon the group began dancing and clapping, enjoying the night. I noticed Cole and Miranda carrying the baby down the path towards the chalets. They were calling it a night. They probably wanted to get Baby Emma to bed, after all it was after ten thirty. I was getting tired myself, it had been a long day and I would have the entire week to enjoy my exotic surroundings. I quietly slipped away and started down the path of leaping lizards and lunging iguanas who were glaring at my stroll towards darkness. Well not complete darkness, a sky of glistening stars watched over me as I neared my chalet home at last. At least this would be home for the next week or so. Upon entering my chalet, I immediately saw all my packed luggage and walked right by it. *No, not tonight,* I thought. I will unpack in the morning and headed straight towards the bed.

"Sweet dreams Asterid," I muttered.

Day Two – May 2nd, 2005

I awoke to the beeping sound of the intercom. At first I forgot where I was. Staring at the canopy through the eyelets of linen, jarred my memory paradise, I was on vacation with a hangover to go with it. The buzzer was not aiding my headache.

The sun was peeking through the bedroom window, probably saying, "Get up, a beautiful day awaits."

I wanted to shout back saying, "Okay, I'm ready."

I got up and ran towards the intercom, but the buzzing had stopped. It just flashed a red light. I pressed the button to call back to the front desk, "Hello."

"Hello," a voice stated. "Miss Asterid, shall I pick you up for breakfast or will you be ordering in today?"

"Neither, thank you. I will skip breakfast Tevin, but thank you just the same," I announced. "I will just make coffee."

"Very well then, I shall be by at eleven thirty to bring you to the main beach area for activities. They begin at noon."

"That will be fine," I said. Though it was not a far walk, I did not want him to feel slighted so I agreed.

It was nine a.m. and if I was going to ever unpack, I had better begin, I figured. But coffee first. I made a cup of joe and went onto the deck to watch the ocean and absorb some sun. While breathing in the fresh ocean blue, I tried to chart my course for the day. First, I will unpack. Then I will head out for my three-mile jog. No need to go astray from my fitness program just because I'm on vacay, it would defeat all the hard work I do at home to stay thin and fit. So, I finished my coffee and went back inside to start unloading the bags. First bag held shampoos, makeup, moisturizers, lotions, soaps, and other toiletries. I tossed them into little white baskets and set that on the vanity in the bedroom. Then was lingerie, bathing suits, and undergarments. I put them in the bureau drawers. The third suitcase had skirts, dresses, and blouses. I had already these on hangers and hung them up in the wardrobe in a corner of the bedroom. Last suitcase was pants, shorts, and yoga wear. These went right in the bureau also. Now shoes, and there were plenty. All kinds of sandals, sneakers and heels, probably won't wear half of them but what the heck, I couldn't decide which to take. I arranged all the shoes on a rack at the bottom of the wardrobe by style. Flip flops, then sneakers, then flats, then heels. I guess I am a bit OCD.

Well, I thought, *mission accomplished. Now I can run.*

I threw on a pair of grey yoga shorts, a white tee, grey sneakers, and threw my hair up in a scrunchie. I started down the dock towards the beach sand and began my run. I ran down a long stretch of beach, staying on the dirt path that paralleled the sifted white sand that blanketed the entire area up to the shoreline. The sun glared, but the tropical winds assisted with cooling the air to just a comfortable temperature, just right. I felt energized. Soon I came to the second chalet which had blue shutters, a beautiful turquoise. Considering the baby stroller on the dock, I would guess this was Cole, Miranda and Emma's quarters.

I had two miles more to go and was feeling great. I could have run the entire island I thought, but I would just stick with my three miles. I wanted to make it to the beach for activities, whatever they may be. I continued on, taking in the view of sparkling white sand and blue sea on my right and the coconut, palm, sea-grape, and ironwood trees. On my left the beauty flowed on and on like the ocean.

As I approached the third chalet, the two-mile mark. The chalets were all about a mile apart. I guessed it belonged to the Reiner's by the toned-down color, it was mauve. Subtle and conservative, that was what mauve is to me anyway. I did not see them though, maybe they were at breakfast.

I assumed I had one more mile to the next chalet, then I could wind down by walking back to mine. Jumping over a few lizards, I continued running, but saw no sight of a fourth chalet. The rest must be on the other side of the island. Soon I noticed a line of tall palm trees perpendicular to me that were not passable. I stopped to walk over to a white sign where the trees met the beach. It read, "Private, please keep out". I sat on the sand and wondered what the sign was about. I sat to catch my breath and after five minutes got up and peeked through the trees.

Beep! Beep! Beep! I turned around to see what all the noise was about. It was Tevin in a yellow dune buggy, yelling, "Miss, Miss are you lost?"

I knew by the voice it was Tevin. He was wearing a blue t-shirt, khakis, and had a big straw hat on his head.

"Oh hello, Tevin." I wondered, *What was he doing here? Probably checking on me.*

He smiled and said, "How did you get all the way down here?"

"Oh, I just went for my morning run. I usually run three miles a day back home! This seemed like a perfect route to take. It is exactly three miles."

As I babbled he interrupted. "Ok come," he said. "I will bring you back to your chalet, Lucas is giving surfing lessons at noon. You have to get ready."

"Oh," I said. *Lucas is activities director,* I remembered.

"Oh yes," he said. "He is a champion swimmer and surfer," he added. The entire time he was looking back at the roadblock of trees, trying to get me away from the area as quick as possible.

I wondered, *why, what was the big mystery? Is that where the older brother was?* Most likely. Though it was out of character for me to pry, I did just that.

"So Tevin," I said as we were cruising down the path, "what is behind the trees back there?"

He said, "Oh, the office and house of Mr. Quenten. He needs his privacy to work, he works very hard. The island runs because of his hard work. He does not like to be disturbed." At that, he stopped at my dock and said, "Ok, here we are, Miss. I will pick you up in one hour."

"Oh no, I will walk Tevin. I enjoy it and the main beach is so close to here."

"Very well, I will be around. If you need me, just call."

"Ok thank you." I jumped out of the jeep or buggy or whatever it was and waved with relief. He seemed so determined to drive me around. Well I cannot say I blame him I was his job, to accommodate me while I was here.

He sped away like a little kid in a go-cart and I headed to my chalet. I was so hot now and sweat dripped in my eyes, so I took refuge in a big cold bottle of water from the fridge and gulped it down with gusto. By then it was eleven o'clock and time was ticking, so I went out to the deck, stripped out of my running gear, and stepped into the shower, still thinking about the man who lived in solitude, the fifth brother. He was definitely gorgeous, at least in the painting, he was mysterious with those crystal bluish green eyes. As I continued dwelling, I realized, he could also be married, with children even, which would be my luck. But what's the difference, I'm not here to find a man, though I would not mind too much if I did!

So, I stopped this pendulum of romantic thoughts and got out of the shower. Rested and revived, I went to the bedroom to retrieve a bathing suit. *Oh my God*, I looked in the drawer. *Which one?* There were dozens, bikinis, one pieces, tankinis, and two pieces. *Oh, I'll just wear the white bikini, it will show off my tan*, I decided. To enhance the look, I took out a white crocheted maxi dress, long and see through, perfect for the beach. I just needed flip flops, the silver ones were calling to me as I opened the wardrobe door. My look was complete, wet hair still but I knew the wind would come to my aid in the drying process. I almost forgot sunglasses, silver of course, and off I went. With a hop, a skip and a jump, so to speak, I arrived at the beach just on time

It was now noontime and the beach was beautiful, an array of rainbow colors contrasted the white sand. There were colorful beach umbrellas on each white lounge chair. The umbrellas were purple, pink, yellow, green, red, blue, and orange. There was a snack bar with colored stools to match the umbrellas and Rupert, in a bright red apron, behind the counter. He was flipping burgers and serving snacks and refreshments.

"Welcome, Miss Asterid," he cheered from his place at the snack bar.

"Hello. Beautiful day," I said.

A big white tent was set up with massage tables and a masseuse standing next to them. I guessed she was there to ease the pain after the surfing lessons. I laughed to myself. A little store stood on the other side of the snack bar and the sign read "Surf Shop". It was painted with wild colored surfboards on it and looked very welcoming.

Two brothers came over to me as I stood in awe, admiring the set up. I did not know which two they were, I just said, "Hi, guys."

"I am Jonas, I am Lucas," they replied with a little giggle. I knew the other was Rupert because it seemed like they all had their own gig and they stuck to it. They all had on white t-shirts and orange, lifeguard-colored shorts.

"Lucas will be giving surf lessons today," Jonas said. He seemed to be the spokesperson. But no, wait a minute, he did speak.

"Miss Asterid, the other guests are in the surf shop choosing their boards. Why not join them?" he said, and so I did.

We entered the shop and "wow" is all I could say. Boards of many sizes, shapes, and colors hung from the wall.

"Name your color. Oh wait," he said and went over to a not so big, purple surfboard. "Is this to your liking?"

I said "yes" immediately and took the board. Maybe I should have taken the bright yellow, I had never surfed before and probably needed to be visible. But purple is bright also so it would do and it is my favorite color.

I noticed that there were some guests missing. I turned to Lucas and asked, "Have all the guests arrived?"

He said, "No, we have the twins and the newlyweds but the others will not be joining us this afternoon."

I could reason with that. The Reiner's were elderly and the other couple have the baby to care for. Lucas interrupted my thoughts for a moment and said with a big white smile. "But we have a great surf out there today. Shall we begin?"

We started out towards the water, all six of us, Lucas in the lead. The water was divine, warm on my legs and waves to enjoy. We began by paddling near shore for the first hour, none of us had surfed before so it was hilarious. We laughed at each other and Lucas laughed too, but continued to encourage us with his bright smile and beautiful blue eyes. His silky hair blowing in the wind, he was a pleasure to the eyes. His diligence finally paid off and after an hour we were all standing and balancing our boards in deeper water. The hot sun and lukewarm water had a balance of their own. It was very refreshing and I was not too hot at all, it felt just the right temperature. It was a fine day and I actually did learn to surf, I was balancing and moving with the waves. But it was very tiring!

"I'm getting out!" I exclaimed. "I need a break and a drink."

Lucas laughed. "Very well," he said. "Go and rest."

The others were getting tired too, so they chose to go for massages over at the massage hut. I declined, I just wanted a drink and a lounge chair. I ran over to the lounge chair where I had placed my towel, put my board down, and sat in relief. The sun was still gleaming, it had to be three o'clock by now.

Before I could decide on what drink I wanted, Jake rushed over with one for me. I wondered how long he had been on the beach, I did not notice him until now.

"Hello Miss, I have a surprise cocktail for you. My own invention, hope you like it."

I sipped it because I knew if I drank too fast, the alcohol would go straight to my head and it was too early for that. "Oh," I said to Jake, "This is delicious. What is it?"

"Fresh fruit juices, oranges, peaches, plums, cherries, and blue curacao."

"No wonder it tastes so good! Thank you Jake. When did you arrive on the beach today?"

"Just moments ago," he said.

"Well cheers." I continued to enjoy my delectable refreshment.

Soon the others joined me and Jake ran right to the tiki bar to accommodate them too with refreshments. As we lay on our chairs, laughing and sipping, Lucas made his way over to us.

"Did everyone enjoy themselves?" he asked.

"Yes!" we all simultaneously exclaimed.

"Good," he said approvingly. "Now if you all will excuse me for a bit, I will collect the boards and put them back."

Again we all simultaneously answered, "Okay."

I think we were a little tipsy from sun, surf, and drinks. Oh well, it felt good to be so relaxed and by now the twins were giggling and staring at Lucas as he walked away. I think they had a crush. Gregory and Georgio were toasting each other. But seeing the twins eyeing Lucas, it reminded me that there was still no sighting of the older brother. He really was a loner, I guess. Sebastian was missing alas, but I supposed he was preparing the entertainment for tonight or just taking the day off. Anyway, it really did not matter, they were all enjoyable people, at least the four I met. So polite, so perfect, so eager to please.

Then a silly thought came over me. *Children of the corn*, I thought. *Oh, Asterid, stop!* I said to myself, or at least I thought I was thinking it and not saying it.

But then everyone looked at me and said, "Stop what?"

I laughed, "Oh nothing, just thinking out loud about something funny."

Maybe they were buzzed because they all started laughing hysterically and I joined them. *Maybe I was buzzed*, I continued. We were having such a fun time when Rupert came over with more burgers.

"Who's still hungry?" he asked. The twins took a burger each and Gregory took two.

Georgio said to him, "Are you still hungry? Will that spoil your dinner?"

"No way," he said, "all that surfing made me famished. I will still be hungry for dinner tonight."

Dinner, I forgot about dinner. I don't know why because I was getting hungry too.

"What is for dinner?" I asked Rupert. He was still nearby and he turned right around.

"Miss Asterid, did you get an itinerary?"

"Maybe," I said. "Probably, but I did not get a chance to read it."

"Oh no worries, well you are in for a delightful surprise. Tonight is the luau right here on the beach. I have been roasting the pig on the chalet patio all day."

"I thought I smelled something delectable, but I thought it was your burgers."

"Yes, maybe that too. Everyone be here by eight tonight because we are going to have such a delightful adventure." Then he walked away, proud and satisfied with the information he shared.

The twins got up and started packing their beach bags and the newlyweds followed their cue. I guessed they had enough sun for the day and so had I.

I found myself falling into a slumber as they all said, "Bye Asterid. See you at the luau."

I said, "Bye, I will see you all in a few hours."

With that, I figured I'd rest a few more minutes. The sun was so warm on my face and the wind was blowing through my hair like fingers of the earth, so content and peaceful I was.

Suddenly, I woke to voices from afar, shuffling noises, and furniture moving and banging like a hammer to an object.

Trying to make sense of my surroundings, and noticing the sun beginning to set, I was just about to get up when my chair began to move. It was the lounge chair, I must have fallen asleep on the beach after the others left. I was moving backwards at a rapid pace. Was I still dreaming or was I awake? No! Someone was pulling my chair!

As I was being pulled faster and faster, holding on for dear life, I yelled, "Stop!"

Too late, I flew off the chair onto the sand!

Just then a man ran over to me, picked me up, and said, "I'm sorry! I did not see you!"

I looked at him as I lay in his arms, those eyes. I thought, *it's him!* The mysterious eyes in the painting!

"You're Quenten!" I said.

"Are you alright?" he said.

"Oh yes," I said, mesmerized by the sight of him. He stared at me and continued holding me. "You can put me down," I said, not really meaning it. "I fell asleep," I added.

He set me down and as I looked around I saw the other brothers shuffling around, preparing for the luau. They were setting tables and long tables, hammering tiki torches into the ground, and hanging decorative lights. Yet still smiling as they worked. They were joyous to observe. Quenten wasn't smiling, he was cautiously waiting to confirm my well-being.

"I'm Asterid," I said to him.

"Nice to make your acquaintance," was all he said, no smile, no frown, just a straight look on his face, very serious. He was very different from his brothers.

Jonas came over at the right time, one could cut the tension with a knife!

Jonas said, "Miss Asterid, you are too early for the luau."

"No Jonas, I never left the beach. I fell asleep and just woke up," I informed him.

"Oh," he said laughing. "Well, go then and get ready. It is six p.m. and the luau will commence in a couple of hours. Do you need transportation to your room? I'll call Tevin for you."

"No, no," I said, "I like walking. I'll be fine."

"No!" Quenten eagerly interrupted. "I will drive you."

He still did not smile but I did not refuse. He was gorgeous just like the painting, even better. He had a buzz hair cut like the painting and the same beautiful green, green eyes. Yet unlike the painting, he had a tint of blue in them and seemed to be built better than what I saw in the picture. He wore faded blue jeans, a light blue cotton shirt unbuttoned all the way, showing his dark tanned skin, and beyond six-pack abs. We walked over to his jeep. He carried my beach bag and helped me get in because it was too high for me, the tires were huge.

"I have not seen you around," I said to him, just to make conversation and perhaps to get some response other than one or two words.

"No, I usually am working down at my place," he said. That's all he said, but he did not have a stern tone. It was softening up a little, just a little. I did not push the issue, regardless of his attitude, tone or whatever. He was gorgeous and I was in his car with him and behind that straight face I sensed some interest in me as well. After all, I was far from ugly, if I do say so myself. He continued driving and I secretly stared at him from the corner of my eye.

We neared my chalet and I was going to tell him it was mine but he pulled over to my dock and said, "Well, this is you."

Sadly, it was. How did he know? I was rather enjoying myself, riding with him. I bet no one else got a ride from him ever. I could only hope.

"Will you manage o.k.?" he asked as he gave me my beach bag.

"Oh yes, thank you, Quenten," I blurted out somewhat trembling, as if the big romance was about to end, and the funny thing was, it was just a ride, a simple ride nothing more. I jumped out, bag in hand, and said, "Goodbye."

I started walking down my dock, heart in hand, that the relationship was over, so to speak. Of course, I was being silly, I knew there was no relationship. I was waiting to hear him drive away, but he didn't instead he stayed there. Should I turn around? No! Don't you dare! I thought and just a I reached the door he left, traveling straight down the path, probably to his place.

I entered my room thirsty, famished, and sun-stricken. I headed right towards the fridge and grabbed a cold bottle of water and some cheese cubes. I figured cheese would hold me over until dinner, though I would rather be sinking my teeth into one of those juicy burgers Rupert was flipping. I should have had one. Well too late, I will have to improvise with the cheese for now.

The water was cooling and refreshing as I drank it and alternated between water and cheese. I started to feel better and very cool. I think I was getting chills from too much sun, so I decided a nice hot bath would suffice. But when I went in the bedroom to get my bath ready, I looked in the mirror and I was scorched, my face and body were beet red! Maybe a cool or lukewarm bath was a better idea.

I drew my bath in my shell shaped tub and added bubble bath. As I submerged into the bubbling clam shell, the aroma and gentle jets soothed me. Yes, the tub was a jacuzzi also.

"Aahhh," I sighed aloud as I succumbed to the warmth and tranquility. I just waded in the water for a while so I could warm up completely and contemplated my outfit for the luau that night.

Beep! Beep! Beep!

It was the intercom and I knew it was Tevin calling to make transportation arrangements for the luau. I was not getting out of the tub to run to the intercom! I figured I would call him back when I was ready. I was thinking the purple romper and tan spaghetti strap sandals would be nice. The romper had white flowers all over it and would fit the Hawaiian theme.

Beep, beep, beep!

Again! I glanced at the clock and it was approaching eight p.m. So, I came out of my shell (no pun intended) and ran to the other room, putting on my robe on the way.

"Hello," I said.

"Hello," said a voice but it wasn't Tevin. If I wasn't mistaken, it was Quenten.

So, playing stupid, I replied, "Hello Tevin!"

He replied, "No, it is Quenten. Will you be needing a ride to dinner? Tevin took ill."

I was shaking all, over partially from excitement and partially from nervousness. Did he want to pick me up because he wanted to see me again? Did he give Tevin the night off in order to do so? Or was Tevin really sick and it was his duty. Probably the latter, his voice lacked enthusiasm, generosity, and persuasion.

"Oh, no thanks. I prefer to walk."

"Ok," he said and hug up.

Oh no, what did I do? This gorgeous guy wanted to pick me up and I said no. Even if he didn't want to, I still could see him again and now I wouldn't. *Good job Asterid*, I thought.

Well, it was not as if I rejected him, I was just reacting spontaneously to the invitation and I was not sure if he really wanted to drive me. My intuition is usually appropriately accurate and if it wasn't this time, he would find a way to see me. Why am getting so caught up in him? *This is my vacation*, I thought, *that cost an enormous amount of money, I should be enjoying it myself and not be worried about some stranger!* I wanted to walk anyway.

I needed a drink, so I took out a bottle of chilled champagne and with a corkscrew on the counter I opened it and began pouring, watching tiny bubbles fizzle in my glass. I drank the tingling liquid right down, tickling my lips and quenching my mind. Refreshing!

As I was putting on my romper, I was thinking maybe I should have accepted the ride. *Enough with the thoughts*, I told myself. My hair was a mess, so I ran for the bottle of dry shampoo and sprayed away. Between the shampoo and curling gel I looked like I just walked out of a salon. I didn't need makeup because the sun took care of that, my beet red cheeks complimented my red strawberry blonde hair and green eyes. By now my thoughts were racing simultaneously with my body, it was getting late and I needed to get to the luau. Sandals on and there I went, scurrying towards the main beach. Legs and mind racing, I arrived.

A tiki torch lit gala awaited my presence. A long picnic table for ten was set and already occupied by nine, so when I sat down at the end the table was complete.

"All present," Jonas exclaimed. "Glad to see you, Miss Asterid."

The others agreed, greeting me also with hellos and smiles.

"Thank you," I said. "I was detained a bit, I think by the champagne in the room."

All laughed and raised their glasses, they understood.

"Cheers," everyone said in unison.

Jonas came over to me and hung a lei around my neck. "Purple, right?" he asked.

"Oh yes," I said, then laughed.

While the other guests were drinking and socializing, I looked around to see if the other brothers were present. Sebastian was over on a platform setting up his instruments: a guitar, a keyboard and a trumpet. *How many instruments does he play?* I wondered. Rupert was standing over a gigantic grill with his utensils, grilling what seemed to be the entire menu!

Jonas and Lucas started carrying platters of food over to the buffet table. I gazed around in awe of my surroundings, a kaleidoscope of edible extravaganza. Hawaiian statues, enormous clay pots of colored flowers on the sand, Hawaiian flowers of orange, blue, yellow and purple, and a path of blinking colored lights which lead down to the water. Even Sebastian's stage and Jake's tiki bar were decorated with colored, blinking lights.

Jake was mixing Mai Tais and Blue Hawaiians. I loved those, they were made with blue curacao, rum, and pineapple juice, decorated with cherries and fancy umbrellas, so I went right over to the tiki bar.

Jake smiled and said, "Which would you prefer, Miss?"

"Oh, a Blue Hawaiian," I said.

"Here you go," he said, and I took my glass back over to the table, noticing that Jake and the brothers all matched. They wore blue Hawaiian shirts and white shorts with tan sandals. All had leis around their necks, very festive. The one thing I didn't notice was Quenten. Again, he was not present! It just bewildered me how different he was from his brothers and the other staff. Not that it was a bad thing. Maybe he was quiet and withdrawn or maybe they were just too happy and outgoing. Who knew?

The group was still chatting and laughing in their Hawaiian outfits. The twins were in purple, yellow, red, and blue mau-maus. The Reiner's in matching Hawaiian shirts, white with blue flowers. The doctor in white khakis and his wife in a white skirt. The newlyweds were in colored tees. Gregory was in yellow, Georgio in orange, and both in Hawaiian shorts. Miranda and baby Emma had matching white and turquoise sundresses and Cole wore a turquoise shirt and white trousers. They all matched too. Sebastian started playing Hawaiian music and the luau was beginning to really take off! Just in time, because I was getting very hungry.

Jonas soon motioned to us to come and over to the buffet table, we all welcomed his cue. I think I made it to the table before the rest and awaiting me was a gallant salad of romaine, baby spinach, strawberries, walnuts, tomatoes, cucumbers, chick peas, red onions, and croutons with raspberry vinaigrette drizzled over it. Then followed green garden veggies grilled to perfection, hot cornbread with butter, poi, and, last but not least, platters of roasted pork, already carved to spare us the trauma of seeing the entire hog hanging on a rack. No, the meat was headless, thank God. Instead we were only subject to slices of pork dressed with smiling pineapples and cherries. An eyeful delight!

I took an oversized pink and yellow flowered plate and covered it with salad, veggies, and pork. The others followed and all plates were filled with the scrumptious fixings of the Hawaiian Islands, prepared for us by our hosts from the Bahama Islands. We sat and enjoyed each bite of the glorious feast, sipping our drinks in between, and listening to Sebastian play. The other three brothers sat with Jake at the tiki bar and ate also. They looked pleased with both the food and our approval of it, probably more pleased with our enjoyment than their own. That's how they seemed anyway. It was a perfect night. The air was serene, the sky was bright and the water sparkled as it slept under the lighted night. All was well in the world as we continued our luau feast.

I noticed Sebastian had joined the others at the tiki bar, but the music still played. He must have put on a record. Yes, a record, I saw a turntable up there on the platform. I recognized the song because my mom used to play it. It was Don Ho, he was singing "Tiny Bubbles". My mom loved Don Ho, she played his music all the time when I was a child. I started to feel saddened by it though, I was still mourning her loss. Though it had been two years since she passed, I had not progressed to thinking of the good memories only. I was still felt despair, despair for her suffering, for my father's loneliness, and for losing my best friend. I felt tears coming so I needed to recluse somewhere. I got up and headed toward the restrooms, wherever that was.

I figured I would walk across the way because they had to be somewhere near the food hut, so I just continued in that direction. I thought I remembered a restroom in the back of the hut near the fountain.

Jonas then sparked his attention toward me and came running over, "Miss Asterid, is everything alright?"

By then I was teary-eyed and I'm sure red nosed, "Oh yes, allergies. I just need the Ladies room."

"Oh, well go right into the dining chalet and it is in the back."

Ok, I thought. So I said to him, "Ok thanks," and continued walking.

He was still talking, "Hurry back, we are going to dance the hula. Hope you will join."

"Oh, I will," I reluctantly said to reassure him, but not reassure myself. I scurried into the chalet and once inside I burst into tears, full blown sobbing! The more I thought about how Mom would have loved this place, the harder I cried like a baby! So sad.

"Are you ok?" a voice echoed from the kitchen area. It surprised me immensely.

"Oh," I said and must have jumped a mile off the floor.

"I'm sorry," the voice said. It was dark inside, only a dim light shone from the corner.

My eyes began to adjust and I could see it was Quenten. He was fixing something, he had a wrench in his hand and looked like he had gotten soot on his face.

"What the hell are you doing sneaking around?" I exclaimed.

He just stood there amazed at my scolding him, mouth agape. But somehow that struck me as funny. So I broke out into a laugh, a continuous laugh and soon he began laughing too. Like two idiots, we continued laughing hysterically and I don't know if I was more shocked at myself or at him. I did not think he ever laughed, but he did. Then I stopped my uncontrollable expulsion and ran across the dining hall into the restroom. I ran into the side that said "Ladies" and launched behind the door, my body pounding like one big pulse. I was so nervous! His presence intimidated, yet excited me.

I paced back and forth in the bathroom, wiping my face and fixing my hair in the mirror. *He must think I'm nuts*, I thought. *How can I go back out there? What will I say to him. I'll stray here all night, then I don't have to face him. No I cannot do that. I'll wait until he leaves. No, he's fixing something. He may be here all night. What will I do?*

Thoughts were going around and around my head, I was a mess. I was getting hives on my neck. *This has to stop*, I thought. So I splashed my face with cool water, took a deep breath, and opened the bathroom door to retreat back to that big room with the mysterious man standing there, probably thinking God knows what. I just kept walking toward the exit and I saw no signs of Quenten. I was almost there when I saw a dark figure near the door, it was him. My heart began to race and I could feel my body trembling. But still trying to keep my composure, I continued toward him. He was astounding even in dirty blue work pants and a white dirty tee.

I was just going to walk past him without saying a word when suddenly, he spoke. "Why were you crying?" he asked abruptly.

Startling me again I jumped, I guess it surprised me that he was being aggressive. Well, for him it seemed aggressive.

My body flowed with emotions of anger, embarrassment, and intrigue all at once and it was telling me to keep walking, yet my mind was saying, *Answer him. This is your chance for that long-awaited encounter with him!* But before I could make any decision, my legs carried me right by him and I ran back across the sand to my seat at the table.

Mrs. Reiner then spoke. "Is everything alright, dear?"

"Oh yes," I said, feeling flushed at thought of having to explain myself to her. "I just needed to use the rest room."

More information than she needed but I had to say something, I did not want her to think we were going to have a heart to heart. The couple with the baby were excusing themselves for the evening. Emma was fidgeting.

"Have a good night all," and off they went into the night. It must have been a long day for a baby. It was a long day for me already and I was not a baby, though I acted like one a few minutes earlier.

The other guests were up on the dance floor. It was not exactly a dance floor, more like an area of beach sand surrounded by lights sticking up from the sand, but it was nice. Hawaiian music played continuously and the brothers lead the group. They were all doing the hula, accompanied by Don Ho's song, "One Paddle Two Paddle". *Yup, that was the name,* I remembered it vividly. Now all were wearing grass skirts over their outfits and, consumed with deliberation and determination, they swayed their hands hips and feet in sync with the brothers who were leading the dance quite divinely.

The celebration looked inviting, though I declined the invitation. Part of me was still in the dining hut, and I just couldn't shake my thoughts of him. By now the Reiner's were dancing too and I was by myself at the table watching. But I then got some unexpected company.

It was Jake, who eloquently spoke. "Miss Asterid," he asked, "Why are you not dancing with the others?" He handed me a Mai Tai.

Maybe I looked like I needed one, so I laughed and said, "Oh, I have to be feeling daring to get up and dance, especially the hula. Maybe this will help," and I took a sip of the delicious cocktail.

To my surprise, he took a seat across from me at the long table and there we sat, just the two of us. It was getting dark, but I could see his white teeth shining as he smiled at me. So I smiled back because I did not know what else to say.

"Miss, may I ask you a question without overstepping?" was his next question.

"Yes, of course," I said, taking a big sip that time.

"I sense sorrow in your face and voice. Is everything okay?"

"I am a little sad, but it's no fault of anyone. You see, my mother died a few years ago and certain things remind me of her that trigger my sadness, like the music and dancing. She loved this music, she would have loved it here. She and my dad probably would be here with me if she were still alive. He is a busy man but he would have come if she wanted to, so that's probably why I am sad. My dad is a lost soul without her, which reminds me. Jake, how can I send a letter to him? Since there are no phone lines."

"Oh that's easy, you can give your letter to Tevin tomorrow and Quenten sends all the mail out by boat to the main island tomorrow night."

"Oh," I said. "Quenten?"

"Yes, he is the older brother."

As he was speaking, I interrupted him and said, "Ok yes, I know the one that hardly smiles and is never around."

His face dropped, "So, you met Quenten."

"Briefly," I said, "But I apologize for the abruptness. I really don't know him. It's just that Lucas, Jonas, Rupert, and Sebastian are always smiling and happy. They attend every event and the other brother does not. It is none of my concern."

"No offense taken, Miss. But something you should know, Quenten created all of this, this paradise for people to come and relax in luxury and seclusion, a vacation of a lifetime. So, if his presence is scarce, it is so the dream can continue. He organizes and oversees all of the day to day events, he handles all monetary business, and he prepares each day for the next with little time for himself. So please do not confuse his being stressed or tired as grouchy," he said.

"No, I was not judging him, just an observation. I think his brothers contribute much to the island. They have certainly helped to make it a paradise They cater to all our needs and are always willing to please!"

I was a bit taken back by Jake's defensiveness for Quenten, but I guess he knew him well and obviously liked him a lot.

Iin his defense again, Jake added, "Quenten would have loved to come tonight, but the oven in the main dining hut broke and it needs to be working by tomorrow so he is making repairs."

I almost said "I know, I saw him," but instead I said, "Well Jake, we all have that rock to roll up the hill. As Camus would say."

Strangely enough, he said, "Yes Miss, but Quenten has four rocks."

He seemed wise. I know he meant well but tonight I was just not myself, so I excused myself. "I am getting tired," I told him and started to leave the table.

I noticed two iguanas across the road hanging out so I went over to the buffet table, grabbed some romaine, and proceeded towards them. They were near the doorway of the dining hut but I assumed Quenten had left, so I was safe. Not safe from harm, just from making a fool out of myself again. I reached the reptiles and held out the lettuce. They must have been hungry because they did not hesitate to snatch it right out of my hand. They were trying to make friends with me, rubbing on my legs and smiling, I think. Well, at least I was making two more friends even if they were of reptile descent. I then heard banging coming from inside the hut and some drilling. Quenten must have been still in there.

Then I heard *thump, thump, thump, thump*. What was that? I thought turns out it was me, my heart was thumping a mile a minute. I needed to calm down. I felt like one big pulse. *Calm down*, I said to myself, *compose yourself and go see him.*

I did just that. I started to the door and the reptiles followed.

"No," I said, "you two wait out here." I didn't know if they understood but they came to a halt. I entered and the noise echoed louder, he must have been behind the big oven so not wanting to alarm him, I shouted a bit. "Hello? Quenten, are you there?"

Silence, no answer but the noise stopped. Then after a few seconds, which seemed like hours later, he rose up from behind the stove and said, "Yes, I'm here," almost with a little excitement in his voice.

That was a good sign, I figured. I moved toward him and could see he was exhausted, like my dad looked after a long, hot day of pouring concrete. I continued closer and was soon right next to him. He had no shirt on now and his work pants were ripped at the thigh, he must have caught them on something. His bare chest and exposed upper thigh excited me! I had to control myself from grabbing him, any part of him or just all of him.

I spoke instead, "Just wanted to apologize for running off before, I don't know what has gotten into me tonight."

"No no, you have nothing to be sorry for, I should be the one apologizing. I knocked you off the chair today and surprised you tonight when you thought the hut was empty. I am sorry."

"No, Quenten," I said. "I snapped at you earlier and I shouldn't have. I guess I am just…"

Before I could speak any more, he put his strong arms around my waist and kissed me, and not just a peck. I mean a long, hard, wet, beautiful kiss. Then I finished my sentence casually, "like I said, I guess I am having a bad night."

I was still in shock from his impulsive kiss. I started kissing him, it lasted for a while, his lips were so tender and we fit together. I think you just know when you fit with someone. This was totally out of character for me and probably for him also, but it was so right.

"That was nice," he said when we stopped.

"Yes it was," I agreed.

We stared into each other's eyes in silence, but we had body language instead. I couldn't move, nor did I want to.

Finally, Quenten interrupted the embrace by saying, "I am actually your ride for the night. Tevin is ill and resting, so I can come back for you if you would like to stay at the luau or are you ready to leave?"

"Oh well, I hope Tevin is ok and I was leaving the luau anyway. I'm tired, so I was just going to walk back to my place. I heard the mail goes out tomorrow night and I wanted to write a letter to my dad."

"Oh," he said, "Ok, well no need to walk. I'm going by your place anyway, I will drive you."

I really did want him to drive me so I could gaze at his gorgeous face all the way, but I did not want him to know that. He packed up his toolbox, shut off the light, and we started to go outside, but the door opened before we got to it and in popped Jonas.

"Oh hello Quenten," he said. Quenten nodded at him and Jonas continued, "Miss Asterid, there you are. I was wondering if you left."

"Oh yes Jonas, I am very tired and wanted to call it a night."

"Very well." He seemed confused about the two of us being together, but he spoke no further.

"Quenten is going to drive me."

"Oh alright," he said. "Good enough, it is unfortunate that Tevin is ill," he said.

"Yes," I agreed. "Hope he gets well soon."

Then with no more words, he left the hut. Quenten seemed fine with giving his brother a nod, as if they always communicated very little. So I guess I was fine with it too.

With blushing red cheeks and toolbox in hand, Quenten looked at me with a faint smile and said, "Shall we go?"

"Yes," I said eagerly, for I was quite happy with that smile, even if it was a little one. He led me around the corner to his Jeep and once again, he helped me up into the seat. I was wondering if Jonas was waiting on my return or if he was suspicious of something going on between me and Quenten. Like a school girl getting caught chewing gum, I began to feel guilty and nothing had really even happened. Just the kiss. The long, wonderful, sexy joining of our mouths and just thinking about it sent chills down my spine.

Quenten got in and began driving toward my chalet and stopped in front of my dock.

"Well this is me," I said, as if he did not know that already.

Then he turned and looked straight in my eyes. "Asterid, come to my place, we can have a glass of wine."

His fiery eyes were insistent and his face glowed under the moonlit sky, making him even more irresistible. I think he liked me or at least was interested in me. I definitely was interested but I knew nothing about him, this antisocial stranger. Somehow I found this intriguing though.

So I said, "Alright, I will come for a glass of wine."

What was I getting myself into? I wondered, *I'm never gonna see him again when this vacation is over, then again that may be a good thing. After all, what fun is being in such a romantic place without romance?*

So, as he drove toward the end of the island, I imagined a secret love affair between the two of us and pretended we were hiding from the others on the island. I hoped my imagination was not going to be more exciting than the reality.

Into the dark we drove, with only the lights of his Jeep guiding us down the path. Soon enough we arrived at the row of palm trees that served as his fence, his no trespassing zone. He turned left into a darker path surrounded by trees and shrubs, so much that one would never know there was a road there. But there was and soon a there was a house or a chalet, rather a huge chalet. This was the big mystery behind the barricade of palm trees that stopped the rest of the world from entering, or at least the rest of the island. His chalet, or villa should I say, was a big structure, well-lit with small white lights outlining the entire chalet like at Christmastime. An enormous stretch of beach stretched before the chalet, miles of white sand and blue ocean with floodlights lighting the beach sand. A paradise within a paradise and no lack of palm trees at that. It was a quite secluded surprise, nothing I could ever imagine. A true pristine picture being cleansed over and over again by the rippling waves of the ocean.

As I gazed at the beauty of the lights enhanced by the light from the stars, Quenten got out of the Jeep and before I could jump out to the sand, he grabbed my waist and elegantly lowered me to the ground. I laughed with delight. He then smiled, not just a grin either, a real smile like one would have if he were enjoying himself. *Was he enjoying himself?*

In the middle of the sand were two large coconut palms about eight feet apart and in the middle, tied to both, was an oversized hammock.

I giggled and asked, "Quenten, is that your bed?"

He laughed and said, "Sometimes, but I do have a real bed inside."

Still looking at the hammock I added, "It looks so enticing."

He grinned and said, "Come, let's go inside. I will show you around and fix you a drink while I shower."

"I think I will try the hammock out and wait for you here, if that's okay," I suggested.

"Of course," he said. "We can take a walk on the beach when I get back."

I nodded and started climbing the hammock which was a bit too high for me so Quenten lifted me up and set me on it. There was even a pillow.

"Thank you," I murmured.

"You are most welcome, beautiful," he whispered.

Everything he did or said excited me in a way I could not understand. It wasn't as if I had never had a boyfriend, just not one who looked like him.

He then turned toward the house, or chalet should I say, and disappeared. I swung on the hammock, gazing up at the stars and moon shining happily in the dark sky. The quiet seemed to be singing to me and the waves clapping with approval of me being there at all, on Quenten's turf.

"I feel much better," a voice echoed from behind me.

It was Quenten returning. He was walking towards me, carrying two cocktails and wearing white knee length shorts and bare chested with that body to long for. My heart was racing at the sight of him. I could not help but be in disbelief that the man I was admiring in a painting a couple of days ago was here with me at his place. Thoughts ran through my head. *Will the night go well? Will he still like me after we get to know each other? Will he pursue me tomorrow? Stop,* I thought, *It's just a man. Besides, whatever happens, no one will ever know.*

He interrupted my thoughts with, "Here is your drink. It's a martini, hope you like it."

"I do," I said. "How did you know?"

"I didn't," he said. "Just hoped you like it."

I took the glass and started to sip. He sipped his. He then laid next to me on the hammock and we continued sipping our refreshments. I started to shiver as his bare skin touched me and he noticed. "Are you cold?" he asked.

"Oh no," I said, "just got a chill from the cold glass, I'm fine."

That being said I kicked off my sandals or at least, tried to. I had forgotten they tied up my leg. He laughed, handed me his drink, and started to untie them. So gentle he was, like he knew what he was doing. I became more and more aroused. I was now gulping my drink and his while he was carefully taking my shoes off and placing them on the sand.

"Thank you," I said. "I was beginning to feel overdressed."

He smiled and took his glass, then said, "Oh, did you want the rest?"

"No, I just got carried away it felt so good. I mean, it tasted so good."

He laughed and his green eyes sparkled and his white teeth glistened. I smiled and sipped what was left of my martini.

"It's so beautiful here," I said and before I could speak another word, Quenten took my empty glass and put it down with his on the sand. Then he started kissing my lips, my face, and my neck. It felt so good, so sexy, so arousing! I was trying to listen to my thoughts because they just ramble on and on but I couldn't even hear them by this time, so I succumbed to him and reciprocated. I started kissing and licking his neck. He tasted so good, like a man should. It's hard to explain what a man should taste like, but he did. I pushed him down and jumped on top of him and continued kissing him, his mouth, his forehead, and his cheeks. He then reached around my neck and untied my romper. I helped by pulling it down for him. Then I started to unzip his shorts, but he just continued undressing me. I was so aroused being disrobed by himn and any skepticism was overcome by the alcohol I consumed and my lust and desire for him. Not to mention I was so horny by this time! I laid on my back, the hammock was swinging back and forth from our movements.

He pulled my romper off my legs and murmured, "You're so beautiful, Asterid."

Next came the thong, which he practically ripped off me. It was white lace, see through. He threw my clothes on the sand and laid back next to me. I finished unzipping his shorts and he pulled them and his briefs off and flung them. My jaw dropped in awe. He was hung like a horse and my expression showed it I'm sure because he grinned with delight at my astonishment.

"Something wrong?" he said sarcastically.

"Wow!" I exclaimed and murmured, "No, nothing's wrong at all,"

After I said that his face turned red. I was beaming from desire and he knew it. He caressed my breasts, kissing my mouth with his soft lips and wet tongue. I squeezed his broad shoulders, sliding my hands down to massage his back. He was now completely on top of me, slowly making his way into me, which I almost dreaded but desired. I knew it would hurt. It was inevitable due to his size. But I wanted him so, both body and soul. Then suddenly he thrust in gently but firmly and that was it.

I thought he had ripped my insides and I let out a big, "Ouch!"

He stopped for a moment and said, "Okay?"

I said, "okay" and wrapped my legs around him and thrust back at him.

I think my hip bones dug into his pelvic area because he looked like he was in pain for a moment, but he endured it as I endured the pleasure and pain comparably. My blood was pumping, my body warm from the inside out. I was in a state of ecstasy and he like a volcano waiting to erupt. I was so excited, I began digging my fingernails into his back taking his skin for my own as he continued kissing, caressing, and thrusting. I consumed him and he did the same to me. I enjoyed him and he knew it. I had my eyes closed for some time and when I opened them I only saw his sparking green eyes smiling into mine. Then it happened, the volcano erupted in a crashing, shattering climax. I felt the warm lava flowing through the valleys of my body! I completely surrendered to him. All of me was his. He moaned and I cried out sweat dripping down both our faces and everywhere else. We laid there, holding each other for hours. We spoke without words. I was complete, he seemed complete too.

Day 3 – May 3rd, 2005

I awoke to a familiar aroma, freshly brewed coffee. I could smell coffee a mile away. I opened my eyes to a sundrenched Quenten standing over me. He was holding a silver tray that supported a silver, steaming pot, two cups, cream and sugar, and utensils. I was covered with a white satin sheet.

"Good morning," he said.

"Good morning. Did we sleep here all night?"

Obviously, I thought, *I was still naked under the sheet.* Then I noticed a white robe laying on the hammock by my side so I hurried to put it on and jumped off the hammock.

He then kissed me and said once again, "Good morning."

All I could wonder was if I had morning breath. He didn't and he was still smiling, so I would leave it at that.

"We both fell asleep out here," he recalled as he placed the tray on a tan blanket on the sand. "Come, I'll pour you a cup," he added.

"Just what I need," I said and joined him. "What time is it?" I asked.

"About eleven a.m. I woke about an hour ago," he said.

He must have showered already because he looked wide awake and shined. He was wearing light blue jeans and a yellow cotton shirt unbuttoned. He always looked sexy no matter what he wore. I liked just looking at him. I could stare for hours, but I wouldn't. He started to fix my coffee.

"Cream and sugar?" he asked.

"Oh yes please, extra, extra."

He laughed, stirred my coffee, and handed it to me in a white cup and saucer. He took his black. We sipped our coffee and waited for the other to say the next word.

All of a sudden we blurted out simultaneously, "Last night was wonderful, beautiful!

"Well," I said, "wonderful."

He said, "Beautiful."

Beautiful sounded more passionate, I should have used that word. But he seemed pleased on the contrary. We both laughed and almost choked on our coffee. I was relieved because he was not the kind of man to say something if he did not mean it and I knew I was being sincere because it was extraordinary.

We stared at each other and then at the ocean. The sun bounced off the water and the water bounced off the sand. The day seemed warm and hopeful, full of ideas.

He then asked, "Are you hungry?"

"No, coffee is fine. But eat if you want."

"No," he said. "I'm not a breakfast person either. Will I see you tonight?" he asked.

It surprised me because there we were after just spending the night together and he was already wondering if he was going to see me. I liked that.

I said, "Well you are my driver, aren't you? Or is Tevin back on the job?"

"I am your driver," he said smiling and continued, "Tevin is off for the rest of the week to rest. I want to see you here again, if that is ok with you."

"Ok. Then you will," I said. He smiled and ran his fingers through my hair as I said, "I must look a mess."

"No," he said, "you are beautiful. Come, I will show you my chalet, it is not quite as large as my brother's but I think you will like it."

His brothers, I thought. This was the first time he even mentioned them, as if they were estranged or maybe I was over-observant. He probably had a good relationship with them and was just busy taking care of the island and there was a big age gap. But I still wondered what Jake meant when he talked about the burdens Quenten had, like rolling four rocks up the hill. It probably was nothing to be concerned about.

So, I started towards the chalet with him and looked around to find my clothes.

"Oh, I hope the robe is fine for now. I washed your clothes, they are hanging on the line to dry."

No dryer, I thought.

But before I said it, he came out with, "I have a washer and dryer. I'm not that primitive. I just figured women do not like their clothes dried, they shrink."

I laughed and said, "You are right about that but the romper would have been fine in the dryer. No worries, thanks."

"You are welcome."

He thinks of everything, I thought. *Maybe he was married once. None of my business really.* I continued onto the porch, through the big wicker door. Yes, it was like my chalet only on steroids.

We entered a big room that was a wonder of copious white. There was a white plush carpeted floor, a white leather sectional that lined three of the four walls, a huge crystal, round table in the center, an enormous crystal chandelier, and white and gold ceiling fans surrounded it to enhance the already well-lit room. The open floor design extended right to the kitchen area with stainless steel appliances on one side and a butcher-block breakfast nook trimmed in white with white leather swivel chairs on the opposite side. It looked so clean and nothing was out of place. I toured the room with admiration and envied his immaculate care.

"Did you design this yourself?" I asked.

"No," he said, "I had a decorator, my only talent is in here. This way," he said and once again took me by the hand and led me through a door off the kitchen.

Still in my white robe, I followed eagerly.

"This is where I get my relaxation," he said. "It may not be much, but it is my art room or rather my painting room. It is probably art to me only."

The room had recessive lighting, multiple easels, and shelves and shelves of supplies such as brushes, cans of paint, turpentine, rags, canvasses, frames, paper, etc. It seemed he had many projects going at once. All of the easels were covered by drop cloths except one that seemed to be freshly painted, but not completed. It was a painting of a large beach, white sand, blue ocean waves, and palm trees. Two trees in particular were very tall and about eight feet apart.

"That's beautiful," I said.

"Thank you, Asterid."

He seemed so sincerely grateful at my compliment, as if he had never gotten one. *This poor man*, I thought, *rather this poor millionaire.* He obviously was all set as far as money goes, but something seemed to be lacking and I could not pinpoint it.

Back to the easel, so he picked up a paintbrush, dipped it in tan or bamboo colored paint, and started to paint a hammock between the trees. I was mesmerized, eager to see what came next.

But that's when he put the brush back in a cup of water and said, "I can finish this later." "Do not stop on my account, you paint beautifully! I enjoy watching you."

I think I just wanted to see if he was going to paint me lying in the hammock or if he was even thinking of that, but I guess I would just let it be for now. Then I thought about the painting in the dining hut and blurted out, "It was you!"

He looked surprised and said, "Excuse me?"

"You painted the canvas in the dining hut. The painting of your family."

"Oh yes," he said, "I painted that when I first came here."

"Oh," I said, "so your parents live here too?"

He just put his head down and said, "No, they don't." Then to change subject of his parents he stated, "I paint by memory. When I finish the hammock, you will be lying on it."

I nudged his arm and laughed. "What?" I asked, "Do you read minds also?"

"No, not all of the time," he said.

I was really beginning to feel comfortable with him, but there was just so much I did not know about him and probably never would. He never asked me about myself, he seemed to live in the moment, which was fine for now.

There is a saying that goes something like, "If you live in the past, you rob yourself of the present. If you forget the past, you rob yourself of the future." I think it was said in Buddhism. Anyway maybe he is robbing his future and I was robbing my present a little. *Oh well, I would enjoy the present for now,* I thought, *or rather, I am enjoying it.*

Still feeling flushed from the idea that he would paint me in his picture, I wondered what was next.

"Come," he said, leading me out of the garage or rather his art room. It could have been a garage though, it was sort of an extension to the rest of the house. We came to a stairway off of the kitchen.

"Oh," I said, "two levels."

"Yes, my office, bedroom, and bathroom are upstairs." Then he looked at me, still in the robe and probably looking pathetic and said, "You can shower if you like."

"I would love to but…"

"Your clothes will be dry shortly and you can write your letter to your dad here," he interrupted before I could give him any reason to decline the offer.

So, I just said, "Okay. But I do not want to disrupt your entire day, I'm sure you have a busy agenda."

"I want you to disrupt my day, Asterid. Besides, I can get some of my work done while you are writing your letter home."

Then, I agreed. His green smiling eyes stared at me with approval as he led me up the stairs.

My heart fluttered from joy and anxiety simultaneously as we climbed the white carpeted stairwell. We arrived at the top of the stairs to a long hallway of white walls and, of course, white carpet.

He continued being my tour guide and narrated as he went along. "The bedroom is on the right, my office is on the left, and the bathroom straight ahead," he said.

With that, I took it upon myself to explore and walked into the room on the left. On the left side was a big wooden desk with papers covering it.

"That's my work area," he explained.

Books filled shelf after shelf along the other three walls and I could not begin to imagine why he needed so many or what they were about. From what I could see, there was about every subject from health issues to politics.

"So many books, have you read all of them?" I asked.

"Practically, I like to keep up on things and, being secluded, I need to read about them."

"That makes sense," I said. "Books are your link to the outside world."

He nodded, agreeing. "Come," he said, "I will show you the rest."

We entered the bathroom, which was lined completely with mirrored walls.

"Oh my God! I do look a mess," I said. My long red hair looked like a short red bee hive. The face looked fine because it was bronzed from the burning sun I had been absorbing for the last two days. The white robe just hung off my stick-like figure but that made me happy. Skinny always did.

"Asterid, you could never look a mess, not even now," he insisted.

I giggled and said, "Oh well. So much for sleepovers."

He laughed. I laughed too because I did not want him to see me as an insecure idiot or something, though it bothered me a bit. He did seem too modest to have mirrored walls. I wondered about it, but did not even ask. I just focused on the tour .

"Do you like it?" he asked.

"Yes, but the walls are very revealing."

"Yes, but I think it is the only place we can see our naked selves," he added.

So I guess what he was trying to say is that he is modest to an extent but not entirely, I could agree with that. But I really need to divert from the subject, maybe I too was modest.

"I love the old-fashioned tub!" I exclaimed. It was in the middle of the bathroom with a curtain surrounding it, supported by a steel rod all around it with an overhead shower attached. It was so big two could fit in it. The tub and curtain were white. I think he did not like colors. There were double sinks on a vanity which consumed one entire wall with the medicine cabinet blending in with the rest of the mirrors.

"Turn on that switch," he insisted.

So, I flipped the switch over the sink and the mirror slid to the side exposing the inside of the medicine cabinet. *Cool!* There was a switch on the other side of the cabinet and I took it upon myself to flip it. To my amazement the entire room lit from invisible lighting that outlined each mirror simultaneously, they could only be seen when they were on.

"What other tricks do you have, Quenten?" I asked.

"Not many," he said. "But open that door," he insisted.

He pointed to a frosted glass door, the kind you would see on a shower. So I walked across the brick floor. It was red brick surprisingly, I opened it was a shower door indeed! I stepped out onto a deck, closed in on all sides, with a square patch of brick on the floor and an open shower above it. Next to the shower was a towel cart holding numerous toiletries. The sun shone directly on the deck and all I thought was, *I'm showering out here for sure.*

"This is great," I said to him.

With that he interrupted my amazement and asked, "Would you like to see the bedroom?"

"Oh yes," I insisted.

So off we went, down the hall again and entered a big room across from the office. "A water bed!" I exclaimed. "I have one too!"

"Really?" he said. "See, we have a lot in common."

I guess we did, we seemed to both be loners. We both seem to like things just so and we probably were both searching for meaning in life. *But for now, I'll just take this moment,* I thought, *for now.* The bed was black epoxy with a shelved head board and drawers underneath each side. It had white satin sheets, very alluring, which made it difficult for me to stop from picturing the two of us rolling around in it.

Since the bed was the only thing in the room I said, "I love the bed."

He was turning redder than red as he answered, "Thank you."

Was he thinking about being in it with me too? I was beginning to feel flushed so I tried to think of something to say. He beat me to it.

"I have some work to do in my office if you would like to shower. Then you can write your letter to your father," he said.

"Oh yes," I agreed. "Your house is beautiful and thank you for the tour, Quenten," I said.

"Thank you, Asterid," he said and kissed me on the cheek.

He was so sweet, not what I expected at all the first time we met. "Oh yes, I would love a shower."

"Well then, okay, everything you will need is in the bathroom and your clothes should be dry, so I will bring them to you."

"Alright, thanks," I said and went on my way. I rushed in and out to the deck, dropped my robe on the floor, eager to take that much-needed shower as I turned on the water, a flow of warmth trickled down my spine. As I lathered up, the soapy suds cleansed my skin and possibly my soul, for I was having no guilt or regrets of the intimate encounter with this sexy, mysterious man I had just met. I felt liberated and proud of my actions, though they were out of character for me. I was seldom spontaneous.

I could have stood there on the warm bricks with the serenity of the warm water flowing on me all day, contemplating thoughts. But I had an entire day and Quenten was waiting for me, so I retreated to the other side of the deck, wrapped myself in a towel, and went to turn the water off, but it turned itself off. *Well,* I thought, *I did not even touch it, must have a sensor. Cool!* I opened the frosted glass and there were my clothes, hanging neatly on a hook on the door. Quenten was just too accommodating, it was sad to think that he didn't have more interaction with the guests. *He makes such a good host,* I thought, *but he probably has enough to do here in his office.* I put on my clothes, the same ones from the night before, but they were clean and I was refreshed just the same. I exited the bathroom, the towel still wrapped around my head in a turban.

I found Quenten in his office, doing paperwork. He turned to me and said, "How was the shower?"

"Rejuvenating," I enthused. "Very, very rejuvenating."

He seemed to be preoccupied and kept looking at a booklet on his desk. The booklet looked like the questionnaire booklet I had to submit in order to vacation here.

He said, "Oh, I'm sorry, I'm not ignoring you. I need to get these reservation acceptances in the mail today. They are for the next group of guests and I'm late on mailing them out as it is."

"Oh, no worries," I said and just as I spoke he got up and walked toward me.

"I will get you some stationary so you can write your letter."

I was feeling a bit intrusive because I could see he had work to do and I felt uneasy interrupting him. I had been here all night and I figured he needed a little space, though I longed to stay forever, I declared, "Quenten, I'm going back to my villa. I will write my letter there and you can work in peace. I know you have a lot to get done and so do I."

At once he was the epitome of loneliness. "Is something wrong?" he asked.

"No," I said, "Nothing is wrong. Nothing is wrong at all." I felt the towel on my head loosening, so I pulled it off and started drying my hair with it that way. I could ease the tension I was feeling and had no more to say to him.

"Alright," he said, "I will drive you back."

He took the towel from me and threw it towards the bathroom where it landed on the floor, but he did not seem to care.

"Thank you," I said and smiled at him

He did not respond or smile back. He reluctantly walked on past me down the hall and down the stairs and I followed, trying to keep up with his fast pace. We headed out the front door and got into his Jeep. He did not even open my door, let alone pick me up and put me in like before.

"Are you mad at me?" I asked.

"No," he said, "I just thought we would spend the day together."

"And we will," I interrupted. "I just wanted to check in at my chalet and get organized. Jonas may call on the intercom to inform me of today's events and see if I need anything. If I am not there what would he think? He does not know I'm here with you."

"Asterid, I can fill you in on today's events. Jonas works for me." He picked up a transmitter radio from the console. "He will call on this," he explained as he held the radio up in front of me. "Jonas also knows I am your driver and caretaker for the rest of the week because of Tevin's illness. So if he needs to get in touch with you, he will call me first."

He sounded like he was hurt by my wanting to leave. There was a sadness in his voice and that is not what I intended. I was flattered that he wanted me there and I wanted to be there, I really did.

"Ok. Then let's get that stationary," I demanded with a smile and a rub on his shoulder. His face began to glow with confidence and I was obliged. He jumped out of the jeep and before I could open the door on my side, he lifted me right out of my seat and carried me back into the house, or villa, or chalet. I was so moved by it all, I was laughing intensely, it made him start to laugh too.

Soon he tripped on the carpet and we both landed on the floor, giggling like children. I closed my eyes to savor the moment and he laid next to me on the floor. Both of us seemed to be recuperating from the laughter and excitement of our little charade.

"Oh boy," he said, "that was fun."

We both gazed at each other for a moment, still lying on the floor, then he blurted out, "I love you."

My heart started pounding, my legs shook nervously, and my ears went deaf to all sounds but my thoughts which were shouting, *Did he say he loved me? Is he joking? Is he crazy? He hardly knows me*! Then before my thoughts could run any wilder, a warm calm came over me. I stopped shaking, my hearing returned, and my heartbeat was in normal rhythm once again, blood flowing quietly. *What happened?* I wondered. His lips happened, they were touching mine and he was on top of me like our bodies had become one and in sync.

I think I did love him, this gorgeous, somewhat shy, gentle but firm, sexy, mysterious/ man. We embraced and kissed for what was only a few moments, yet could have been an eternity.

I was relieved he kissed me before I could answer him, but I wondered if that is why he did it. Could he have sensed the shock of it all to me or did he mean that he loved me as a friend and not as a lover and felt awkward himself. *No, that 'I love you' was real*, I thought, *Or was it*?

I jumped up, and said generously, "So, where is that stationary?"

"I'll get it," he said and he ran up the stairs.

He seemed fine, not embarrassed or anything, so I guess I was fine too. He was back in a couple of minutes, paper, envelope, and pen in hand.

"Better start writing," he said with a big smile, and added, "I'll make some coffee for us."

"Wonderful," I said, "just what I was hoping."

Holding the stationary, I walked over and sat on the couch and put the paper and envelope on the coffee table. The stationary was white with gold trim and the heading on both the paper and the envelopes read "Skinner's Cay" in beautiful scroll. I called to him in the kitchen area, "Nice stationary."

He laughed and said, "Glad you like it," as he continued diligently brewing the coffee.

Then I jokingly asked, "What's for lunch?"

He stopped what he was doing and looked at me, coffee scooper in hand, and said as a matter of fact like, "You definitely do not eat lunch, you weigh three pounds."

"No, I weigh ninety-three pounds," I corrected him sarcastically. "But you are right, I do not eat lunch."

He grinned and nodded proudly to have hit the nail on the head! I laughed and began my letter:

Dear Dad,

I miss you, though only three days have passed. Wish you were here, but with your busy schedule, I understand. My cordial hosts and pleasant fellow vacationers are making this vacation very pleasant. Today...

I stopped writing and called Quenten, "What are the…"

Then I noticed he was right beside me holding a silver tray in his hands. On it was a carafe, sugar bowl, creamer, and a coffee cup and spoon. He placed the tray on the coffee table in front of me.

"Thank you," I said.

"You're welcome, now what were you going to ask me?"

"Oh," I said. "What are the activities for today?"

"I know you know what they are," he said. "Jet skiing with Lucas."

"And the dinner itinerary?" I added.

"Rupert's beef barn," he wittily remarked.

"Okay, thanks." I was amused by his ability to make fun.

He then mixed my coffee for me, gave me a kiss on the forehead and said, "Enjoy, I will be upstairs in my office if you need anything."

"Thank you, Quenten, for everything," I said.

"Asterid, I'm so glad you decided to stay," he said with a sincerity I have never seen in a man before. I just smiled and went back to my letter, but not before watching him walk away. I could not resist that butt and those arms and everything about his physique. Back to the paper, I continued with the letter:

Today we are going to jet ski at the main beach. I'm so excited! Dinner tonight will be themed "Rupert's beef barn." Guess we are having steaks! Sounds so good, doesn't it? Well, whatever they are serving I know it will be enticing and I will surely indulge! Take care of yourself, Dad. I will see you soon,

Love always,
Asterid.

I then placed the letter in the envelope and addressed it:

Mr. William Matteo
11 Stonehill Lane, Providence, R.I. 12908

It was so sad to see the envelope read "Mr." only and not "Mr. and Mrs.". Two years and I still cringe at the thought of excluding my mom from everything except my thoughts and memories of her. She was beautiful, loving, and exhilarating. She could endure hardship, welcomed any challenge, and most of all enjoyed every moment of life. She endured everything but the cancer, that is. Anyway, I know she would not approve of my mourning all the time, I just could not help it.

I sat back on the sofa to enjoy my cup of coffee, reflecting on the events that had taken place over the last fifteen hours. I then realized that a happiness came over me that I had not felt in a very long time. A happiness I longed for but never seemed to obtain until now. This may be my time for happiness.

"How is the letter coming?" I heard a voice calling from on top of the stairs.

"Fine," I said.

"How's the coffee?" he added.

"How are you doing?" I asked.

He mimicked me by answering, "Fine."

"Very funny," I said.

He said no more, he must have returned to his work. I just sat there staring at the empty walls in front of me and wondered, *were these empty walls hiding the past or preparing for the future?* It really was none of my business. Besides, I was just passing through and, so far, enjoying the ride. I started to wonder about the time, it must have been close to three o'clock and my letter needed to be sent out so my dad would receive it before I got home.

Soon I heard the thumping of Quenten coming down the stairs, he had a burlap sack in his hands and picked up my letter. He tried to be discreet about looking at the address, but I caught his glimpse and maybe a sadness in his face when he saw "Mr." only on the envelope. I'm sure he knew whatever I wrote on the questionnaire anyway, so I was not bothered by his knowing about my mom and knowing anything else about me as I'm sure he already does. He never asked questions about my life, so I reciprocated. When and if he was ready to talk about himself, I'm sure he would. At least I hoped he would.

As he dropped my letter in the sack, he smiled and said, "Shall we go drop off the mail?"

"Yes, alright but where do we drop it off?"

"The drivers all collect the mail from their guests and they bring it to me to take to the ferry. The ferry arrives about four p.m. at the main dock."

"Oh," I said.

"Unless you would rather be dropped off at your chalet to get ready for dinner tonight."

"Oh," I said, but it sounded like more of a question.

"Dinner with me. That is, if you would like?"

Like? I thought. "I could eat you right now," is what I wanted to say, but I didn't. Besides, that was not what he meant. He really meant dinner. So my knees started shaking and even knocking together like the time I volunteered to sing at mass and the organist started playing the wrong song, a song I had never heard of. But I sang it anyway and my knees knocked the entire time. I actually did ok. Nobody else realized it was the wrong song, but the knees knew! Well the knees knew again that I was pretending to be calm about the dinner invite. Really I was anxious, nervous, and overjoyed at the same time!

"Yes!" I finally answered, "I would love to have dinner with you."

"Good," he said. "Let's go."

I glided behind him toward his Jeep and again he picked me up like I was a little kid and placed me on the seat. I loved the way he did that, with one arm even. He then went around to the other side, threw the mail sack in the back, and hopped in himself. He pulled me closer to him and his warm body made mine begin to tingle.

"Here we go," he happily announced and we drove off through the path of trees that led to the main road.

We drove down the main road a few miles toward my villa. The sun beamed down on our heads like a reminder of its existence. It was extremely hot, yet a tropical breeze intervened every now and again enabling the palm trees to wave as we passed them. I looked around as we drove.

Not a soul was to be found between my place and his, yet the silence was overcome by the sounds of nature and its force. Then we stopped moving, we had arrived at my place. I was home or at least, my home temporarily. I just sat there in the Jeep, my body still close to his, savoring the moment.

"Asterid, Asterid, are you alright?"

I was in a daze, but soon came to and answered quickly, "Oh yes, I'm fine."

"Well, looks like we are here."

I slid over to open the door and he pulled me back to his side. He began kissing me and holding me tight. We continued the kissing for a few minutes and then he stopped and reluctantly said, "I have to get to the ferry. What time should I pick you up for dinner?"

"Oh, anytime you are ready, I can be ready. I can be ready, Quenten," I said.

As I looked in his deep blue eyes, I was thinking *I could fall in love with this man*. But I deterred from that thought immediately, I hardly knew him and he hardly knew me. He must have meant he loved me as a friend, everyone says "I love you" to people they really like, right?

"What?" he said.

"Oops!" I had said that right out loud, "Nothing, just thinking out loud. I meant that will be fine, the time, you said."

"But I didn't say a time."

"Oh, ok."

"Then how about six?"

"Six is good for me," I said and then he sped off down the road.

I turned toward my chalet and stated skipping down the dark path, thinking, *he was so sweet and I was so smitten!*

I entered the chalet and retreated to the bedroom, straight toward the welcoming canopy bed. I laid there reflecting on the day's events and the events to come. Quenten was gorgeous, sexy, and a great lover, but I could not stop wondering what could really evolve from our relationship. *Fun, that's what!* I always believed that if a relationship was not fun, no matter how loving, it did not last. At least for me it has always been like that. I laid on the bed a few minutes more, though I started to get tired and probably could have dozed off. I got up to see how I could make myself pretty for dinner with Quenten. I took a seat at the vanity and looked in the mirror. *Oh goodness*, I thought. To my surprise my face was red as a lobster! I guess I did not realize how strong the tropical sun could be. Slacking on the sunscreen probably was not helping, but it did look good and I definitely needed no makeup. *Well, perhaps a little shimmer,* I thought and since the bottle was right in front of me, I applied some to my face and neck.

Better, I thought. When I looked up at the mirror my face was glowing. The hair was a different story. It was wild! I could fix it. The advantage of air drying was that my red curls were spiraling, I just needed to fix them. I pinned up my hair to a half up do, ran my fingers through the curls left hanging, and sprayed a little hairspray on them. *Looks good!* I was talking to myself as I anticipated Quenten's arrival.

I figured I needed to find something sexy yet subtle to wear, so I headed to the wardrobe. I recovered my fishnet yellow one-piece bathing suit, with a built-in bra of course, my sheer yellow tint wrap-around skirt, and my metallic gold thong sandals.

As I was about to dress, I heard *buzzz, buzz*. The intercom! I threw the clothes on the bed and ran to answer. I figured it was Quenten, even though it was still early.

"Hello," I said.

"Hello, Miss Asterid. This is Jonas, will you be joining us this evening at Rupert's Beef Barn?"

I did not know what to say. He knew Quenten was my driver and Quenten had to go up near the main house to drop the mail off. I was certain they had crossed paths, or maybe they had not talked all day. I did not know if it was okay to tell him I was dining with Quenten, or if I even should be.

"I will call you back, Jonas. I am in the middle of something right now, that's all," I said and he was fine with that answer. It was good for me because I really did not want to say the wrong thing.

Still flabbergasted, I went over to the kitchen drawer and reached for my cell phone. I wanted to check the time, it was later than I thought. It was almost five p.m. But Quenten was not due for another hour. I guess I laid down for more than a few minutes. I returned to the bedroom and got dressed. The outfit looked perfect on me, I thought and since we were probably dining on the beach I was equipped for a swim too. I admired myself in the mirror for a few seconds. Earrings, I forgot earrings. I had a quaint pair of diamonds I like to wear for dressing up. I took my little jewelry box from the drawer, found them, and put them on. *Oh, very nice*, I thought. Small, but shiny. I was ready so I figured I would have a glass of champagne and sit outside on the deck. Drink in hand, I ventured out.

As I sat in the lounger, I sipped my drink and gazed out at the vast, panoramic ocean in front of me. The ocean waves clashed with the rays of the sun, dispersing an osmotic sparkle. It was hypnotic as I soothed my soul watching the ocean, time was not of the essence. I was relaxed and content so I just sat and took it all in. The sun was strong, I could feel it burning my face after a while sitting there. I wondered how long I had been out there, so reluctantly I got up from the lounge to go inside and see what time it was. When I checked my cell, it was quarter past six. Where was Quenten? He had not even called. Maybe he got detained with the mail or maybe there was a problem in the kitchen. *Maybe he was helping his brothers with something*, I thought. *It's fine.*

I was getting hungry. I did not know if I should have a snack. I did not want to ruin my dinner but if Quenten was tied up or dawdling somewhere, God knows what time I would eat! All of a sudden I heard a strange noise. It was coming from outside as if it were on the ocean. I returned to the deck to see what it was.

It was a boat, a great big boat! All I could tell for sure is that it was white and it was coming toward me. She looked beautiful as she dipped into the welcoming waves of the waves of the deep, diligently staying on course.as she neared. I was stifled to realize it was Quenten driving!

Beautiful! That's what they were, the boat and Quenten. The boat soon pulled right up to my deck and he turned off the motor. With an enticing smile, Quenten asked, "Want a ride, beautiful lady?"

With a smile I answered willingly, "Absolutely" and climbed aboard the white boat with an emerald green stripe on each side and big green scroll letter that read "The Lilly Ann."

I studied the writing as I was making my way on board.

Quenten then blurted out, "That was my mother's name, Lilly Ann. This used to be my father's boat."

He used the word "was" when referring to his parents. *So sad*, I thought.

After a few solemn moments I looked at him and compassionately said, "My mother's name was Ann."

He nodded with an understanding look in his eyes and we both proceeded to reflect, not asking any questions of each other. I decided to sit on the white cushiony seat. I guess one would call it the passenger's seats.

I sunk right in it, it was comfortable and big. It could fit three or four people and there was another on the opposite side.

Quenten approached me quickly, put his hand out, and said, "Come sit up here by my side." I took his hand and followed him to the front of the boat. Before I could sit, he turned to me, put his arms around me, and said, "You are gorgeous, Asterid!"

It took no time in returning the sentiment. I looked at him straight in his deep blue eyes and said, "And you are gorgeous!"

He then kissed me so tenderly, so long, so romantically I could have melted in his arms. My knees wobbled and my heart felt like it was exploding! *I could fall in love with him,* I thought or was I already in love with him? How could that be? I knew so little of him. His past, his family, does he even like his brothers, did something happen between them to distance them from him? How did his parents die? Are they even dead? I felt compelled to learn more about him and yearned to be with him.

He seemed to be luring my heart into his soul, his mind, and his body. Speaking of body, his pecs were bursting, he was shirtless with white swim trunks and was barefoot. *What a man,* I thought. His arms were bulging among other things and he had not only a six pack he had the whole case!

"Asterid! Asterid!" He interrupted my daydream. "Are you alright?"

"I'm fine," I said. "No, I'm better than fine. I'm great," I said as I sat in my seat and smiled.

He started the boat and we plunged into the waves with great speed. My stomach tickled with each rise of the boat into the waves. I laughed and he watched me approvingly.

"It's so beautiful!" I exclaimed.

"Yes, it is," he agreed. Endless miles of blue ocean surrounded the only boat challenging it, Quenten's boat.

The sun graciously followed us on our journey to who knows where? I could still see the island on our left, we would soon pass it by to only the water ahead for miles. We continued cruising the coastal body of blue which housed millions of iridescent fish of all sizes and colors, swimming in spacious schools of symmetry. I took in the view with each breath, admiring my surroundings and my satisfaction seemed to satisfy my captain. Quenten shifted his race mode from high speed to neutral and soon the boat came to a complete halt.

"Thirsty?" he asked.

"Very," I said.

"Come, let's sit on the sun deck," he said. We walked to the stern of the boat and he stopped to open up a storage bin under one of the seats. There was actually a little refrigerator in it. He asked, "What's your pleasure? I have wine, champagne, beer?"

"Water," I interrupted.

"Water it is!" he exclaimed. He took out two bottles of spring water and continued to the deck. We stood at the rails of the deck, gazing at the sea, and replenishing ourselves. It was so beautiful!

Then I said to Quenten, "This is amazing, you must love living here!"

"I do now," he said as he looked at me. He had a very serious look on his face.

I said, "Well I love it here!"

I smiled and we toasted our water bottles and finished drinking. I did not want to ask him why he used the word now, but I hoped he meant that he loved it there now that I was there. A girl could only hope that she was reason for a man's happiness, especially this man.

Quenten gazed into the water as I gazed at him.

"Look," he said. I looked and saw a beautiful school of fish, colorful like a rainbow, swimming in harmony.

"Oh, they look delicious! I mean delightful!" I stated.

He laughed and asked, "Are you hungry?"

"Yes," I said. "I am starving, I haven't eaten all day." I continued, "I guess that's why the fish look so good."

"Good enough," he said, "let's go." He headed toward the bow of the boat and I followed, wondering what was next on his agenda. He sat at the wheel and I took comfort next to him in my seat. He started the engine and diligently took off! We sailed off into the sunset to I had no idea where. There was not a patch of land to be seen, let alone a restaurant, so I assumed he knew where to get food. Maybe he was going to fish for it and have a hibachi on the boat. I thought that certainly would make sense, we had all this ocean so there was certainly no shortage of fish. I figured he was taking me to his favorite fishing spot, but then I saw it. A big patch of land. An island and it was not Skinner's Cay. There were green trees and white sand. It was secluded, waiting for us to arrive. Quenten pulled up to a small dock and turned off the engine.

"How did you find this?" I asked.

"I own it," he said. "This one and a few others I purchased, but this one is my favorite."

I became more impressed with him, if that was possible, everything about him. He had already impressed me immensely. He lifted me up onto the dock and went to the cabinets under the passenger's seats. From them, he removed a picnic basket and a cooler and jumped onto the dock.

"Oh! I almost forgot," he said, "the anchor."

He jumped back into the boat and threw the anchor overboard. "There," he said, with a sexy smile and a sense of satisfaction. I obliged him with a smile also and accompanied him down the dock towards the beach sand.

The entire island only measured about fifty feet in diameter. It was filled with beautiful palm trees hovering over the white sand and swaying in the breeze. The sand received the gentle ripples of the surf the ocean, bidding farewell as the surf receded. I found myself being drawn in by it all and embracing it with my body, mind, and soul. Walking toward the water, I kicked off my sandals so that I too would receive the ripple effects of the warm current. The palm fronds whispered in the soft tropical breeze, I enjoyed it as much they did. Quenten was still carrying the basket and cooler.

I turned and said to him, "Oh Quenten, let me help."

"No, no," he said. "I've got this, you enjoy." He placed down the basket and cooler on the sand and joined me by my side. As we stared out to sea, he said, "This is my paradise away from paradise."

"Yes, it is," I agreed.

He then took out a blue plaid flannel blanket from the basket and spread it out on the beach. "Sit and relax," he insisted, so I did. "Enjoy the view," he added.

That was easy because the ocean circled us and, whichever way I looked, there it was. As I rested under the sun, Quenten busied himself with unpacking the picnic basket. He took out several containers, plates, silverware, glasses, linen, and, last but not least, a mini charcoal grill! The little grill stood on the sand. It had a grate and was already filled with charcoal. Quenten moved it further away from the blanket, for precaution I assumed, and he continued on with his duties, so it seemed. I watched the spontaneous flexing of his muscles with each of his movements and he was a sight to savor!

He was walking back and forth, carrying containers from the basket over to the grill and each time he came toward me he looked at me watching him and winked at me. *Oh, I could melt,* I thought and that was pretty out of character for me. I never needed or desired approval from a man as much as I needed, or rather wanted, his. He was soon done with the food preparation. He took a match to the grill and flames began to rise. He began cooking his well-prepared feast of thick, marinated angus steaks, mushrooms, and onions. He then went to the cooler, took out a big salad bowl of fresh collards and tomatoes and a bottle of bubbly.

I took the glasses and bottle from him and said, "Let me!"

Then I poured the champagne and he put the already dressed salad into two bowls and served it to me.

"First, a toast," I said, "to you, Quenten, for doing all this for me."

He looked so humble and said, "You are welcome, Asterid,"

We drank wine and ate salad and we were happy, so happy. I ate the bowl of greens so fast the fork could not keep up with my mouth. I was so hungry and it tasted so good. I crunched the greens until they were gone.

"More?" Quenten asked, laughing as he watched me devour.

"Yes," I said, "more is good."

I usually wasn't a big eater but once I am hungry, I am hungry. He scooped more greens into my bowl and I continued to eat.

"I'd better check on the steaks," he said and walked over to grill. He flipped the beef and attended to the onions and mushrooms that had been grilling as well. Then he plated the feast. He had two big, white ceramic platters and the food consumed almost the entire plate. One for each of us. Dishes in hand, he made his way back to me, placed the platters down on the blanket, and handed me utensils and linens.

"That looks delicious, I cannot wait to eat it. Thank you Quenten, you have done all this work for me."

"For us," he corrected.

I agreed. "Very well then, for us."

He seemed so happy to be with me, like it had been a long time since he had a date or any female companionship. That was understandable though, I guess he busied himself with running the resort and did not have time for relationships. Whatever the case, I was sure of one thing, I was going to eat this gigantic, juicy steak.

"Let's eat," I said and we did. I started cutting the tender meat smothered in mushrooms, onions, and its own juices and it melted in my mouth. "Delicious!" I told him.

"I'm glad you like it," he said laughing and ate, but I still had him beat. I finished my entire plate and he was still working on his. I sipped more wine and Quenten finished his dish.

The stars brightened as the night darkened and the waves splashed ashore, encouraging a perfectly harmonious atmosphere. We conversed silently with our eyes, continued drinking wine, and absorbed the ocean air.

I interrupted the moment and said, "I'll clean up," and started to gather the dishes.

Quenten took my arm and pulled me down on to the blanket and said, "Leave everything for now."

He rolled on me and started kissing me endlessly. I was hugging and kissing him back and hoping the night would never end. We laid on the blanket staring at the stars as we slipped into a gentle slumber.

Day Four – May 4th, 2005

I awoke to the smell of fresh brewing coffee, or did I? Maybe I was still dreaming, so I raised my head up and saw that I was still laying on the blanket surrounded by white sand blowing easily around, marking its territory on everything, including me. I stood up, still feeling groggy, my hair blowing in my face, and made my way over to the aroma. A pewter coffee pot perking on the grill awaited me. Two cups set on the sand were waiting to be filled.

"Good morning," I heard a voice say from afar. Quenten.

"What are you doing?" I asked.

"Taking a morning swim. Cream and sugar are in the cooler," he yelled to me.

"Thank you," I yelled back with a giggle. I was pleased to see him, but at that moment happier with my cup of joe. I fixed my coffee and sat back on the blanket. *Refreshing,* I thought as I took that first sip and observed Quenten swimming in the sea. The sun reflected vibrantly off the glistening ocean casting a silhouette of his chiseled figure. He swam vigorously back and forth through the waves. He was a pleasure to watch.

I could no longer stand the anticipation of joining him, so I took one more sip of my coffee, removed my wrap-around skirt, and, in my yellow mesh swimsuit, ran into the water. I dove in head first and swam out until I reached him. He embraced me and pulled me close to him and we bobbed in the water like the waves, frolicking like a couple of sleek seals. It felt so revitalized and being with him was a bonus. He was a breath of fresh air, a new outlook on life. He was fun and that made me wonder if I ever really knew what fun was.

We splashed in the splendid, sparkling sea and stole sweet kisses in between. Suddenly, he splashed me right in the face. I was taken back for a moment because he wasn't usually that abrupt, maybe he was becoming comfortable around me.

"You asked for it!" I exclaimed. I let him have one big splash in his face and, after the surprised look he had, he started to laugh and swam after me.

"You are in for it now," he said, so I swam faster and faster for the shore, giggling as I tried to escape him. We both continued swimming and laughing toward shore.

He soon caught up to me and grabbed me yelling, "I love you."

I laughed and soon realized that he was not kidding. He was not laughing any more, but I continued to because I did not know how to react, nor was I prepared to. I did not react. I just plummeted head first into the ocean and kept going, figuring I could sort this out with a dive.

I kept swimming like a fish with a disarray of thoughts. *I think I love this man, but it is too soon for love, or is it?* It was definitely too soon for sex and we already had that, so maybe thinks were going accordingly or, not accordingly, but it's too late for that. It felt so right, he felt so right, and back up I swam. It was either that or drown.

I soared up to the surface and blurted out, "I love you too!"

He sighed with relief. "Thank God," he said and then hugged me tight like a python squeezing its prey.

I couldn't breathe but I never felt better in my life. I loved him and wanted him and he felt the same.

We gazed into one another's eyes for what seemed to be an endless moment and then..,

Buzz, buzz, buzz.

The sound was coming from his boat.

"What is that?" I asked.

"Just my transmitter radio," he answered in an annoyed response. Then he said, "In other words, it is Jonas!"

"Jonas?" I said. "Oh my God! He must be looking for me!"

Quenten looked at me with a smirk and added, "No, I took care of that. He thinks you wanted a private, three day tour with me, so he would have no reason to worry. I know what he wants."

"What?" I asked.

"We have a business meeting every Thursday for resort planning, upcoming tourists, and so. It usually starts at one p.m. so it must be around that time now. I forgot all about it. I will let him know I will be a little late. I'm sorry to cut our day short, but I will make it up to you tonight if that is okay with you."

I was a little disappointed because I thought, *what is the big deal if he missed one meeting?* He could certainly re-schedule, but I supposed I would survive so I resounded, "Of course, I'll help you pack up."

So, we swam to shore and I ran to the blanket, but he ran right to the boat. I packed the cooler and the picnic basket and I heard Quenten on his radio. He looked so sexy on that boat, with no shirt and smiling at me from afar as he spoke to his brother. The sun captured his sparkling eyes and tan body, I couldn't help gaze at him as I continued to pack up. He ran back down to the blanket and joined me, picking up the grill and taking the cooler and basket from my arms.

"Are you upset with me?" he asked.

"No, I understand," I said, though I was a little. "I will see you after your meeting," I added.

"Thank you, Asterid. I love being with you," he said with sincerity.

"Me too!"

We headed back to Skinner's Cay and we approached my deck in about an hour. The ride was quiet, neither of us spoke the entire trip, which seemed a bit awkward but maybe we were both out of words at this point.

Quenten jumped out of the boat first to help me get off. He took me by the waist and lifted me up onto the deck.

"Thank you," I murmured.

He kissed me quickly and jumped back aboard. "I'll call you in a little while," he said.

"Ok!" I exclaimed and with that he waved, blew the horn, and disappeared into thin air. I was still waving even after he was no longer visible, pondering about the wonder of this important meeting. I entered my chalet and went immediately to the couch to lie down. The sun, wind, and sand had taken its toll on me. I felt wiped out!

I laid there wondering how the most defining moment of our relationship could be interrupted with a beep of a transmitter radio. Nevertheless, I needed a shower. Still dressed in yesterday's clothes and feeling quite sweaty, I turned on the shower head but turned it off quickly. A nice bath is what I desired, with lots of bubbles. That would make me feel better. I turned on the tub faucet and poured in half the bottle of bubble bath that was on the shelf. I threw my yellow swimsuit and wrap-around skirt combo on the floor and jumped in to soak my disgruntled thoughts away.

I do not know why this feeling of rejection hung over me. After all, Quenten did declare his love to me and has given me no reason to doubt it. I also declared my love to him and I should leave it at that. He just seemed so impervious to the mention of his brothers at first and now he was rushing to get to his meeting with them. I wondered, *why? Why the change of heart? Forget that,* I thought and continued to soak in my soothing bubbles of calm. The day was still young and I was going to make the most of it. I submerged my face and head in the water, maybe to cleanse my brain from its negative thoughts and came up for a breather. I soaked for about an hour and, though hesitant to retreat from the bath because it was so soothing, I got out and wrapped up in a soft white towel. I got one to wrap around my head too and then laid down, sprawled out on the bed. I was relaxed and refreshed now.

The sun peeked through the shutters from the window on the left wall, reminding me that there was plenty of daylight out there. So, I rose quickly and went to the dresser to get a comfortable outfit to wear. I figured since I had missed my run for about two days, I would take a nice, long walk. I took my Victoria's Secret pink, terrycloth jogging outfit and a pink, lace-trimmed tank top out of the drawer and placed them on the bed. I dried off and took the towel off my head to let my hair air dry. Then I got dressed, pink underwear and bra to match. I was a matchy-matchy kind of girl. I should try to get away from that, but why stop a good habit. Off I went out the side door and up the deck to begin my stroll.

I started walking and thinking good thoughts. I thought about how I loved my time with Quenten. I loved Quenten and, furthermore, he loved me! Love does come first! I knew so little about him, but that seemed irrelevant. Maybe he never talked about his family and his past because he was the kind of person who only lived in the present, which was new ground for me. I dwelled on the past, obsessed with the future, and merely existed in the present. Not a peaceful way of life, I realized. I walked down the path along the beach, the same path I took for my run. I was surrounded by the beautiful blue ocean, blue sky, coconut palms, scampering lizards and iguanas, and sugar white sand. I found myself walking faster and faster to the gentle ocean breeze blowing through my hair. As I neared the end of my route, I saw the sign. That notorious sign that read "private." I was there, Quenten's property. I stopped and turned to go back, but something made me wander over to the path that led to his chalet. There I was, going right up the path even though I knew I shouldn't. I just wanted to peek through the trees and see what was going on. I got to the entrance and tried to see if anyone was around but only saw the chalet and the ocean. I did not have a clear view, so I walked closer behind the chalet where I would not be spotted. I couldn't believe I was really doing this. I usually minded my own business. It was so hot outside, I doubted if anyone would conduct a meeting out in the scorching sun. They were probably inside where it was cool. *Yes of course they were.* I turned to leave and just then I heard voices, voices coming from the front of the house! I peeked around the side of the building and I could see them. It was Quenten and his four brothers. Quenten was standing up in front of them, the other seated in folding chairs with notebooks in their hands, prancing like a kitten preparing to pounce on its prey. I got closer to the edge of the house and had a clear view of them. I think I really just wanted to get another glimpse of Quenten. I seemed to be addicted to him. I missed him already and it had only been a couple of hours since he dropped me off. *One more look and I would head back,* I thought. I listened carefully to try to hear what was being said and it seemed to me that they were reading.

Then I heard Quenten say, "Very good, Rupert. Now Sebastian, let us all hear your new sentence."

Then Sebastian read a line. It went, "The piano was on the stage waiting for someone to a-a-…a…"

Quenten interrupted him and said, "Accompany."

Sebastian continued, "Accompany it."

"Very good," Quenten commended him. Then Jonas started reading, but I had heard enough. He was teaching them to read, but why? *Were they illiterate?* I wondered, *in this day and age*? They were all so well spoken, I found it hard to believe that they never learned to read. It was disheartening, so I turned to make my way back to the path.

I tiptoed gently to the back of the house again and started to run when I heard a voice say, "Asterid!" It was him, Quenten! I was caught in the act, as they say.

"Hi," I said, "I… I…"

He interrupted me and said, "Now you sound like them." He wasn't laughing or kidding and I knew what he meant. He continued, "What are you doing here?" Not in an angry nor a happy tone, but a disappointed tone. He knew I was spying on them, he knew I was listening to them, and he knew I heard them!

"I was just taking a walk and found myself thinking about seeing you and wondering if your meeting was finished so I…"

He interrupted me again, "Well it is not finished, so I guess I should be getting back to it." Then just turned and walked away like a betrayed soul or even worse like a dismayed child.

I had no words nor did I want to speak. I just headed back to my chalet, teary eyed and confused. My thoughts raced as I walked faster and faster. What went wrong in their lives and not in Quenten's? They are thirty years old and cannot complete a sentence. It made no sense to me and probably never will because he is probably finished with me. I really screwed up by sneaking over there. I could have just walked over and let them see me. That would have given Quenten a chance to tell me the meeting was still in session and he would call me when it was finished, or maybe he would have been happy to see me and said, "Come join us, we are just about done." He could have pretended it was a real company meeting and I would have never known the truth, but I did know the truth. As the wheels turned in my head, my sadness turned to anger.

He has problems, I thought. He is responsible for four grown men who appear to be more like children. That must be what Jake meant when he said, "Quenten has four rocks to roll up the hill." Well, I would never ask him and Camus certainly cannot help. I reached my chalet and went inside. *Wine*, I thought and took a bottle from the shelf, opened it, and drank right from the bottle, swigging it down like a drunk off the wagon. I needed it and to sit and calm down. I tried to relax, which was useless.

Then I realized, I have only two days left of vacation. I hardly knew these people, the Skinners, and possibly I have confused love with lust and normal for new. I decided not to question the events of the day any further, it did not concern me. I have known Quenten for only four days and yes, we were intimate, more than I care to admit. But contrary to the fact that I think I love him and he loved me, where would our relationship really go? He lives on a secluded island with the "Stepford" brothers or "Children of the Corn" or whatever one would call them. I was being mean and not liking it and regardless of their past or any explanation, I was leaving in three days, never to return. It would have been a fairytale if things worked out differently but the path not traveled was not for me. Well, the wine kicked in and I began sobbing uncontrollably. I sobbed so much, I was exhausted.

I awoke from the sleep I must have settled into and saw that the sun was going down and the room had become darker. A strong cool breeze was causing the shutters to flap and the room got very noisy and a bit chilly. I must have slept about three hours. I got up to shut the windows and suddenly I heard the intercom buzzing and buzzing and buzzing. Maybe my head was buzzing from the wine. I did feel woozy, disoriented, and in doldrums. Not knowing if Quenten was really mad at me and was taunting me and the fact that he had cut our day short for a meeting that was actually not a meeting, but a kindergarten class agitated me, but I missed him! I missed his warm touch, his soft tones, and his brief smiles and grins, far from the look he had when he caught me spying on him. I just wanted to get that look out of my head.

I figured it was about eight o'clock, considering the sun had completely set. The wind rose and the waves began crashing on the beach. One starts to know the time by the movements of nature on this island. *That's how Quenten does it*, I thought. He never needs a watch or a clock to tell time. Nevertheless, I checked my phone and I was close. It was 8:15 p.m. I was close and so was my stomach, rumbling and growling with rebellion. I knew it would not surrender to anything but food. I was in fact hungry and the fruit and cheese in the kitchen would not suffice.

I headed to the bathroom to wash my face and brush my teeth so I could change and head out to dinner. I really needed food, my clothes were getting bigger as I got smaller. I stripped and looked in the mirror and two hip bones looked back at me. Don't get me wrong, I loved being thin but enough was enough. *I'm going to pig out tonight*, I thought. I picked out a long, flowered-dress that was pink, orange and yellow. I know sounds hideous, it wasn't! It was silky and flowy, came down to my ankles, and had ruffles around the neck and sleeves. It was very cute and I had the perfect yellow flats to go with it, patent leather. I dressed into my attire and started to fix my hair, when *knock, knock, knock*, at my door.

Oh my God! I thought, *is it Quenten?* I ran as fast as I could to open the door and it was just Tevin. He was standing there, smiling with a big picnic basket. "Good evening, Miss, I have your dinner." He lifted the basket a little to show me.

"Oh, Tevin, I thought you were ill, so I was just about to walk up to the dining area!"

I was thinking, *where is Quenten?* I was angry, for certain he got Tevin out of bed to bring me dinner.

"I was sick, but I am feeling much better. When Mr. King asked me to fill in for him because he was now feeling ill, I was happy to oblige."

"Well I think I will go to the dining hut just the same," I said. "Mr. King?"

"Yes," he said, "or perhaps Mr. Quenten to you."

"No, perhaps Mr. Skinner. At least that's what I thought his name was...this is Skinner's Cay. Am I right?"

He laughed, "Oh yes you are most certainly correct, but that is just the name of the island."

"Oh," I said in a state of confusion.

He decided to leave it at that. Then he interrupted my confusion by saying, "Dining was in-room tonight, today was siesta-fiesta Thursday did you not get the memo?"

I said, "Oh yes, I did but I must have forgotten."

What memo? I thought. But then again I have not been here much the last couple of days, so that would explain me missing the memo. I think Tevin could tell I was agitated and it was not his fault. I did not want him to think I was mad at him so I tried to lighten up a bit and said, "Tevin, thank you for dinner and you should go and rest."

"Oh," he said laughing, "Thank you, Miss. Enjoy." Off he went into the night and off I went to the table to put my big basket down.

I opened the basket to a savory mélange of cuisine and a delectable aroma. There were rows of colors and shapes like a candy assortment. There was a row of beautiful tacos, they seemed to be filled with steak, chicken, and ground beef. One of each, dressed with shredded lettuce, carrots, and tomatoes and topped with sour cream, shredded cheese, and salsa. There was another row of quesadillas with stir fried steak, onions, and mushrooms topped with what seemed to be a combination of shredded cheeses. There were different kinds of beans placed in little tins in the last row for the sides. White linen napkins were rolled up with silverware inside them and tucked in neatly at the end of the assortment. This looked divine and I dug in. I started with the quesadillas which were delicious. They melted in my mouth and I kept eating until I devoured two. I then tried some fried red beans and though I'm not a big fan, the beans were quite tasty. I figured I had room for one taco, so I chose the chicken and started it. But I thought I'd get up and get a bottle of water from the fridge. I drank the water and thought, *King, his name is Quenten King.* Maybe Skinner was his mother's maiden name. Well, what did it matter? It was not my concern.

    The meal was great and the day was done and there I was all dressed up and it was time to go to bed. I left the basket of satisfaction on the table and went to the welcoming canopy in the bedroom to lie down and reminisce. Reminisce about the good part of the day when Quenten and I were swimming splashing and loving.

Day 5 – May 5th, 2005

I awoke with a tremendous headache. I was hungover from food, wine, and grief. The room was dark. Not even a sliver of sun sprinkled through the shutters of the windows. I wondered if it was still night. I was still dressed in my clothes and I had not heard from Tevin. Usually the intercom would be buzzing if it was morning and as far as I knew it did not buzz yet. I managed to drag myself out of bed and made it over to the window. It was daylight alright. Though dark and dreary was the weather, I could tell it was time to rise. Coffee, that is just what I needed to get a jump start on my day. So I went to the kitchen and brewed a nice hot cup, taking in the aroma as I waited patiently to pour. As I stood at the counter I thought, *if only I could call my dad, I would have someone to vent to.* I missed him. We usually had our coffee together in the morning at home before work and got caught up on things from the day before because we were both too tired at night to converse. We both put in long demanding hours. Then I thought some more about calling him and figured maybe that would not be such a good idea. I would probably spill my guts and he would say, "Asterid, just come home and get away from those crazy people!"

He said it as he saw it. So the non-contact situation was probably a good thing in disguise. Oh well, my coffee was brewed. I poured it in my cup, mixed in my cream and sugar, and sat down at the dinette to consume it. I sipped while staring at the basket I left at the table the night before and wondered what the activities would be for the day. It didn't appear to be much of a beach day. In fact, it looked like rain.

I ventured out to the deck to see how the weather really was and it was quite warm outside, though gloomy. I sat in the lounger and watched the waves rising higher and higher before crashing to a defeat of ocean. I felt calm for some reason, calmer than they were. It occurred to me that if the ocean could find harmony in some way, so could I and everything works out the way it should one way or another. I finished my brew and decided to go inside and begin my day. My headache was subsiding and I was now awake.

I still had not heard from Tevin, which was unusual but maybe he figured he would let me sleep in since it was a cloudy day or maybe the activities were cancelled due to the weather. *I will just get dressed and go to the main beach and find out for myself,* I thought and so I commenced with my plans. I went to the bathroom and took off the dress I had on from last night and matching undergarments and decided today is a new day. *Maybe I won't even match,* I thought. *Time for a change.* I turned the shower head on and stood in my clamshell tub and took comfort in the warm water pouring out of the spout of purification. I lathered up and shampooed my hair vigorously and it felt good, refreshing.

When I was finished and clean I got out, wrapped up in my towels, one on my body and one on my head of course. I went to the wardrobe and contemplated my attire. *What shall I wear?* I wondered. I saw a divine terrycloth set. It was black and white, black beach pants with white trimmed pockets and drawstring and a matching zip up hoodie. So, I decided to change it up and get the aqua hoodie from another outfit and wear that with the black pants. I thought of the aqua tankini I had and rummaged through the bathing suit draw to retrieve it. *Perfect,* I thought. *I now have a mismatched matching outfit.* So I got dressed. I looked in the mirror to see what had to be done with my face and hair, but I alleviated that problem quickly. My face was so tanned and burned I just needed moisturizer and I thought two pony tails would be different for my do. I was good at ponytails. They were easy to put in, two elastics and I was good to go. I got my white Keds out of the shoe bag, slipped them on, and headed for the door. I saw the basket of food I had on the dinette and figured I would bring it with me to give to Rupert. I did not want it hanging around in my kitchen. I took the basket and started out the door and ventured down the deck to begin my adventure for the day.

A gloomy adventure it would be, I thought. Even the palm trees were drooping and the sky seemed dark, the low clouds treetop high, it seemed. Not a bird or a person to be seen is what I noticed while walking toward the main beach. I wondered if everyone was at the beach already and started the activities. It could not be later than noon, so I continued my journey with one goal in mind, getting there and trying to have fun. Yes, Quenten was in the back of my mind, hanging there like a dull headache that would not let go. I started to wonder, *where is he?* At his place probably, pretending to be ill. He will probably "be ill" until I depart. *Just as well. I just hope I can fit in with the others since I have not been around the past few days,* I thought. Then I arrived at the main beach area and it was abandoned. No one was around.

"Where is everyone?" I said aloud to myself I guess.

"They are out on the fishing boat with Lucas!" a voice exclaimed.

It was Jake, wearing a white t-shirt and khakis, carrying bottles of liquor to the tiki bar, where I was standing in astonishment for I had missed the boat, literally.

"Hello, Miss Asterid."

"Hello, Jake. I thought activities were at noon, so I came up here figuring I was on time but it must be later."

"No Miss, you are on time. But due to weather conditions they decided to go out earlier. Tevin tried to call you several times this morning but when he got no answer, he assumed that you were sleeping in. What is that you have, Miss?" he asked as I stood there looking foolish and holding the big basket on my arm.

"Oh," I said, "this is the basket from last night that Tevin brought me. The fiesta was delicious but I was not able to finish it all."

At that moment Rupert came running out of the food chalet, "I will take the basket, Miss."

"Oh hello, Rupert." I hoped it was Rupert. I assumed it was him because he was the foodie.

I was right because he said, "Hello, Miss Asterid. I see you missed the others. I am sorry!"

"Oh no, that is nobody's fault except mine. I overslept and I missed Tevin's calls."

"Well," he said, "today is 'Rupert's Fried Friday' and whatever fish the guests and Lucas catch, I will fry. Why don't I cook you a burger for now? There will be plenty of fish for you also tonight, so no worries."

Then Jake added, "And I will fix you a drink."

"Oh no, guys, I am not hungry, thanks. I would just love a cup of coffee," I said to Jake.

"Very well, I will put on a fresh pot. Take a seat," he said as he pointed to one of the stools at the bar. So I did just that.

Rupert took the basket from me and said, "I will be in the hut preparing vegetables and sauces for the fish tonight if you need anything, Miss."

Off he went and Jake followed to get the coffee pot, I assumed.

So, there I was by myself, sitting and wondering what I was going to do for the rest of the day. I thought maybe I would tour the other side of the island where the twin's and the honeymooner's chalets were. There was a beach on that side also that I had not seen. *Yes, that would probably take up some of my time and I would not have to go anywhere near Quenten's place,* I thought. But I wanted to and I wanted to very much. I just wanted to see him, look at him, and maybe I would be satisfied and I could go on with my day happily. *That was so absurd,* I assured myself, *if he ever sees me spying again that would be it. What does it matter?* I figured, *he does not want to see me anyway.*

"Here we are," said Jake as he walked toward me carrying a silver tray. On it was a coffee pot, creamer, and sugar bowl. He placed it down in front of me and then took a cup, saucer, and spoon from a shelf under the bar.

He then got a cup for himself, he came over to place it down. He poured mine and then one for himself.

"I will join you, Miss Asterid. I have plenty of time on my hands, the others will not be returning for a while," he informed me.

"Oh great," I said. "It smells so good."

I fixed my coffee and he started drinking. "You have it black?" I said.

"Oh yes," he said, "Always." He watched me adding one hundred sugars and a gallon of cream. "You like yours white?" he said with a grin.

We both laughed because mine was totally white and looked like a cup of milk. "What time is it?" I asked him.

He looked at his watch, which was a fossil, and said, "Just about one o'clock."

Then I asked, "Did everyone except Rupert and you go fishing?"

"Oh yes," he said.

Still prying, I asked, "Even Jonas and Sebastian?"

"Yes, it's a big boat."

I think I was hoping he would say something about Quenten, but he just sipped his coffee and smiled. The day seemed to be getting darker and my mood was equivalent. I sipped my coffee and Jake started slicing lemons and limes and putting them into little bamboo bowls.

"Is the fish fry outside tonight?" I asked.

"Well that depends on the weather, it certainly looks like rain. We were not expecting any for this week, but you never know on an island," he said.

A few minutes later, Rupert came out of the food hut carrying a basket and came over to the tiki bar and with a big smile placed it in front of Jake and me.

"Your lunch is served!" he exclaimed. There were two enormous burgers and a bushel of fries in it and the aroma was just calling out to me.

I really was not thinking of food until I saw the feast, "Oh Rupert, it looks so delicious."

"Yes, it does," Jake agreed.

Then I added, "Please join us, Rupert."

"Oh no Miss. Thank you, but I have much preparation for this evening."

"Are you sure? There are only the three of us here, we should enjoy it," I said.

"I am quite sure, Miss. But thank you for the invitation. If you will excuse me I will go, just call me if you need anything at all," he added. He went back to his hut and Jake and I dug in. Jake even sat down as if we were dining together.

We bit into our delectable burgers like they were filet mignon, they probably were. They were so delicious. I could not tell what spices he used, but the flavor was incredibly addicting, I could not stop. Jake looked happy too.

I think Jake was hungry and needed to eat because after a few big burger bites, he started talking so much as if someone plugged him in. "So, Miss Asterid have you enjoyed your vacation thus far? Is everything to your liking? I hope we have accommodated all your needs."

"Yes and yes"

Then we both laughed and continued eating our meal.

"Rupert is such a talented chef and so delighted to please, as are his other three brothers. They are so motivated, they never miss a beat. They never falter. Do they, Jake?"

I left out the part about their little reading deficiency because I was not going to delve into their personal problems with Jake or anyone for that matter.

Jake looked surprised at my observation and said, "Oh Miss, yes they are very deliberate and basically happy but we all falter. It is the human condition." Then he laughed a little, mostly to himself and popped a fry into his mouth.

I was still thinking of his sentence and the word condition kept flashing in front of my mind. "Conditioning!" I yelled.

"What?" he asked.

I did not realize I was yelling aloud and he looked so taken by surprise, I said, "Oh nothing, I was just thinking out loud about something. You are right, we all falter. Let's just eat."

Jake resumed eating and I resumed drinking my coffee. I was so full, I could not eat one more bite. I just wanted to concentrate on my hypothesis. Now the psychologist in me was kicking in for the first time during this vacation. I thought about the name of the island, Skinner's Cay. Skinner was obviously a name which showed ownership in its context. The only Skinner I have ever heard of was B.F. Skinner the scientist and not just because I studied psychology. Everyone who has ever studied at a college has heard of Skinner and his discovery of operant conditioning. He believed people could be conditioned to certain behavior by teaching through reward and punishment. He wrote a book titled "Walden Two" in which a community of people joined together to form the perfect society, the perfect utopia, through the idea that certain behaviors were acceptable and certain behaviors were not. Skinner even experimented on his own child for a period of time. He kept the child in a controlled environment that he called his "Skinner's Box." I started to wonder, *was this island a big Skinner's box or a small Walden? Is that why the quadruplets were so matter of fact in their actions and behaviors? Is that why the island is considered to be the perfect paradise? Even more, is that why the brothers could not read or were just learning to read at the age of thirty? Was Quenten behind all of this? Is that really what this is or is my imagination running wild?*

I decided to stop thinking crazy thoughts because with Quenten nowhere in sight and Jake not mentioning anything about him, as if he disappeared off of the face of the earth, the romance of the last few days were fading fast. It was like being in a dream and now I was awake. Maybe it was all a dream, a long beautiful dream. One that I never wanted to end, but reality does bite and it bites hard. I started to feel little drops of rain and Jake did too.

"Well, I guess it is going to rain after all," he said as he took the last bite of his burger. "We have been lucky so far Miss, haven't we?" he asked.

"Oh yes, we have had beautiful weather so far," I said. "Now Jake, I think I will take this basket back in to Rupert." I did not want to make Jake clean up and I figured Rupert was busy preparing the evening's 'feast'.

"Oh no," he said. "You are a guest. No work for you while you are visiting us. I will bring this inside," he said as he took the basket from me.

"Alright then," I agreed to let him because there was going to be no arguing this cause and I smiled. He went on his merry way and I sat there wondering. Wondering when the fishing expedition would be returning. Wondering if I should just go back to my chalet and start packing for my departure even though it was not until two more days. I just felt stuck between a rock and a hard place. The whole thing with Quenten was up in the air and I felt out of place with the rest of the guests because I had been AWOL for most of the time. I felt like I did not belong with the other guests or with Quenten.

Just then I heard a low rumbling noise. An engine sound, like a vehicle. Low and behold it was! I saw Quenten pull up to the food hut and park his Jeep. He did not notice me sitting at the tiki bar and that was a good thing. I did not want to face him. I was not prepared. What would I say? What would he say? I was not ready for that yet. I missed him. I longed to be back in his arms, feeling his embrace, and embracing him. I missed his soft lips against mine and his hard body against my tiny one. *Oh, even if he is a mad scientist,* I thought, *he's a sexy one.*

He got out of the jeep and did not look my way. I sighed with relief and ducked down a little, but I could still see him walking towards the doorway of the hut. He was wearing dark blue jeans and a dark green shirt and kept walking until he reached the door and went inside. *I have to make my getaway now*, I thought. So, I ran toward the path and kept running down the road toward my chalet. I did not hear anyone or anything so I stopped and turned around. I was in the clear, no one was behind me. They were probably all still inside. I continued down the path and soon reached my quarters. Down the dock again and into the door to which has become my meager existence, hiding away in my chalet on the ocean.

This was not what I planned. I sat down on the sofa in the dark, I had not even opened the shutters so the room was gloomy, just like the day. I started to get comfortable on the sofa, relaxing and trying to put my thoughts on hold and it was working well. I reached a comfortable zone in my mind and tried to keep it there and I actually started to feel better. I thought about the fish fry and was looking forward to mingling with the others again. They were easy people to mingle with I guess and all had their own agendas. I figured they were not concerned that I had not joined them for a few days, after all everyone has the right to do their own thing. *Yes, I think it will be fun*, I thought.

As I sat and stared into space and enjoyed the peacefulness I had set in motion, all was disrupted by a loud noise coming down the road. *Oh no, it sounds like Quenten's Jeep!* I thought, and it was.

"He was probably just on his way to his place, relax," I said to myself out loud. I was sure he would drive by and all would be well again. I would be able to relax once more. But he did not ride by. I heard the engine stop, so I peeked through the shutters and there he was getting out of the Jeep and heading down the dock. He was coming to my door and there it was, *knock, knock, knock*. I sat silently on the sofa with no movement, hoping he would just leave and at the same time excited that he was there. I thought he was done with me and for whatever reason there he was knocking at my door. He did want to see me, but why? I thought maybe Jake told him I was at the tiki bar when he arrived there and then I was gone. But he had all last night and this morning to try to see me and he did not, so why the big hurry now? He was not concerned with my whereabouts before, so I think I will not answer the door, I decided.

I did miss him and my heart fluttered with the thought of him, yet I was still angry and confused about everything like about his brothers learning to read, about his past being so secretive, and about the mystery of Skinners' Cay itself. Was I just imagining all this or was something not right? I could be making a mountain out of a mole hill, but I have always had good instincts and trusted them. I just did not know anymore.

"Asterid, Asterid," he called my name and knocked.

I just sat still and kept quiet.

"Asterid, are you there?" he continued, but I remained frozen.

Then I heard footsteps going down the dock. I let out a big breath of relief as I heard him start the engine and drive away. But when I peeked through the shutters, I noticed he was turning his vehicle around and heading back toward the main beach. *Was he going there again to look for me? No, probably not,* I thought. *He probably had to help Rupert set up for the fish fry tonight,* I assumed.

At that moment, I decided not to dwell on things any longer. I closed my eyes and rested in the dark room. It was actually comforting, to be shielded by the walls of dark finite where no one could find me, not even Quenten. I thought about nothing, nothing at all and it seemed to work. My mind cleared up and my body surrendered to the stress-free environment of the moment. Life was good again. It was mine and nobody else's. The dark became my friend and my blank thoughts gave me hope again. This was the meditation I…

Buzz, buzz, buzz.

Well that was short lived, I said to myself. The intercom was buzzing and I was deciding whether or not to answer it.

Buzz, buzz, buzz, buzz, buzz

They were persistent. *Who could be trying to reach me?* I wondered. Not Quenten. I hoped it was Tevin. The fishing expedition had probably returned by now and he was calling to inform me about the fish fry this evening. The one I already knew about. I rose from the sofa and went over to the intercom to be ready to answer it if it buzzed again. Nothing, the intercom remained silent as I did I. *Maybe it wasn't Tevin, maybe it was Quenten again trying to contact me,* I thought and returned to the sofa to try to get back to my zen place, so to speak.

Buzz, buzz, buzz, buzz.

The intercom was buzzing again full force. So I ran to it and said, "Hello."

"Hello Miss," a cheery voice responded.

"Hi Tevin," I quickly said.

He hesitated for a moment as if he were surprised that I answered. I guess he was getting used to me not responding. "Good to hear you, Miss," he said.

"Thank you Tevin. How was the fishing trip?" I asked.

"It was nice, we caught lots of fish, Miss. Sorry you were not there. Will you be coming to the fish fry?"

"Oh yes, I would not miss it, especially after all of your hard work today catching the fish."

He laughed and said, "Very well, I will pick you up at seven. Is that alright?"

"Seven is fine," I agreed.

With that he said, "Goodbye," and was soon off the intercom.

I was still standing there looking at it as if there was something more, but there was not anything more, at least nothing more for either one of us to say.

I knew it was time to get out of the tub because my hands were shriveling up, so I rose, shut the running water off, and grabbed a towel to wrap around me. I forgot to take the ponytails out, so the ends were wet. *Oh heck*, I thought, *I will blow dry and straighten my hair tonight*. I was tired of the natural, wavy look anyway. I then realized I had not had any alcohol at all since I woke up. Towel still in place, I moseyed on to the kitchen, took out a glass, and opened the fridge. *What shall I drink?* I asked myself. The champagne looked inviting, so I poured and poured until my glass was full and bubbling. Then I gulped it down because I was so thirsty to begin with. I had nothing but coffee to drink all day. It tasted so good and refreshing, I poured another glass and drank like I was in the desert and had come across the first stream.

I now felt better and ambitious. What was I thinking, not having a cocktail all day? It was vacation and I liked cocktails, why don't I drink at home? This is when I answered myself, *it makes you feel too good Asterid*. I could have gone for a third, but I needed to get dressed and finish getting pretty by the time Tevin arrives. So off to the bedroom I went and put on my robe so I could start my hair and makeup. I removed the elastics from my hair and retrieved my entire cosmetic case from the closet, along with my blow-dryer and straightening iron. I applied moisturizer to my face and then a light radiant foundation to give it a little glow. Then I did my eyes. I liked brown eye shadow, so I blended three subtle shades to give my eyes a natural look. The brown shades enhanced my green eyes and made them look very green, like a cat at night. Then I applied black mascara, a bit of green eyeliner, a bronzed blush, and a tawny lipstick. *Beautiful*, I thought and it smelled so good. I loved the smell of good makeup, like the smell of a cosmetic counter in a department store. To me it smelled better than a perfume counter.

With my eyes glowing and my face sparkling, I went on to the hair. I plugged the curling iron in to heat it while I used the blow-dryer. With a round brush I dried my entire head so it would be smooth enough to straighten easily. I had a lot of waves in this head. It took about fifteen minutes to get it straight, pulling it with the brush as it dried. Straightening was easier. The straightening iron glided through it like a hot spatula on the frosting of a cake. *My face and hair are done,* I thought as I looked in the vanity mirror, I just needed to dress and I would be ready. So, I proceeded to the bureau, opened the draws and decided, light blue skinny jeans and a white, semi see-through blouse. I pulled out a tan bra and tan lace panties, put them on, and then dressed into the jeans and blouse. Then I thought, *I have denim espadrilles. They will match my jeans perfectly.* So, I went to the closet and took them out. As I put the shoes on, I was wondering if I forgot anything. *Earrings*, I thought. *I'll wear my diamonds that were my mother's I had put them in a little case in my suitcase and I left them in there. I did not want to lose them. I knew which suitcase because I put them in the smallest one. I retrieved them quickly and put them in my ears. I was finished.* I looked in the mirror and saw a beautiful woman standing there. I was feeling like myself again, confident and optimistic.

I was hoping it was close to seven and Tevin would be arriving because I was ready to go, not that I was hungry. That burger that Rupert made this afternoon was still with me. *It was so delicious and filling,* I thought. Well I needed it and the mirror says so. I stood in front of it again and confirmed my suspicions. I have lost weight, I probably weigh eighty pounds by now. I even missed some of my runs and I have still lost weight.

Knock, knock, knock, I heard coming from the other room.

"Miss Asterid, are you there?" It was Tevin.

Great, I would not have to ponder any longer. *He is here and I was ready to go*, I was thinking as I ran to the door to greet him. "Hi Tevin," I said with a big smile.

"Hello, Miss," he said with a smile back. He added, "I am a few minutes early, hope that is fine with you."

"Yes, of course," I reassured him and off we went to his little buggy to the fish fry. I noticed Tevin was looking a bit drab in a white, stained t-shirt, dirty looking blue jeans and sneakers, and there was a smell in the buggy, fish. He smelled like fish.

I guess he noticed my awareness of the smell because he turned to me and said, "I was helping Rupert clean and prepare the fish. You always decline a ride, Miss Asterid, so I did not shower and change before I picked you up. Sorry about my appearance and smell, I will shower when I drop you off."

I laughed and said, "No worries, Tevin. I do always decline, I was just feeling bad about never accepting a ride. I love to walk, I would have walked tonight if I knew you were busy."

"Oh no Miss, you are my priority. I am here to serve you first." He was so sincere, I actually felt bad.

As we approached the main beach area, I noticed bright white lights, like a big castle. It was a big white canopy that occupied most of the beach and it was lit up like a pyramid.

"That's beautiful," I said.

Tevin smiled. "Yes, Mr. Quenten did all this, he always participates in the fish fry and makes an appearance to greet the guests. He also helps with the frying, I guess it his way of thanking everyone for coming to his island," he said.

"Great!" I said as I started to panic. I did not know Quenten would be here, nor was I ready to see him.

I tried to compose myself, but I guess I was not doing a good job because I just sat there until finally, Tevin said, "Ok, Miss, we are here." I guess he was waiting for me to get out but I still sat there in a fog "Miss Asterid?"

I jumped out suddenly and said, "Thank you for the ride," as calmly as I could and proceeded toward the tiki bar, without taking notice of anyone or anything that was part of my surroundings.

I did notice Jake with a glass in his hand. "Miss Asterid, how about a pina colada?" he asked.

"How about Jack Daniels?" I said.

"Straight?" he asked.

"No, with Coke will be fine."

"Very well," he said and started to fix my drink. I refrained from looking around. I did not want to be seen by Quenten, but I guess it would be only a matter of time before he would notice me. Jake handed me my drink and I sipped it, probably so I would take a long time finishing it. The longer I prevailed, the safer I was, I figured.

I was doomed, I thought. *It would only be a matter of time before someone approached me*, I realized. *I had better get my act together and join in on the festivities*, I thought and one more sip helped me along. I turned around to look at the gathering and I saw a big, white brick fire pit in the middle of the tent. It was beautiful and held a big grate of frying pans, big black frying pans filled with fabulous foods, fish mainly.

The aura of the flames from the fire pit drew me in so, I failed to notice its surroundings. There was a beautiful set up of little white picnic tables all around the pit with white wooden chairs to match. In the middle of each table was a big pineapple center-piece and a pitcher of what looked like red sangria with lots of fruit floating around in it. It was lovely.

There was just one thing missing, people! Where was everyone?

Suddenly, Jake was saying my name, "Miss Asterid, Miss Asterid."

I was so busy looking at the dining area, I failed to hear him trying to get my attention.

"Yes, Jake what is it?" I think I was a bit abrupt because he interrupted my thoughts but he paid no mind to my tone, I guess he was used to dealing with all kinds of people.

"The others are inside getting their souvenirs. Would you like to go in?"

"Souvenirs!" Interrupted by the sounds of laughter, we both turned toward the dining hut as a parade of yellow came thundering out the door. It was the other guests and they were all wearing yellow rain parkas. Jake and I looked in amazement.

I could not resist saying, "Is there a yellow raincoat convention?"

We both laughed hysterically. I think my giddiness had a lot to do with alcohol consumption and his was just good humor!"/

"Those are the souvenirs!" he said still giggling and I watched as they marched out of the hut like they had just won the lottery. They all were wearing jeans which was surprising because I did not think that Doctor And Mrs. Reiner even owned a pair of jeans. They all wore sneakers too. *I guess they have a dress down Friday all over*, I thought. Then out came the brothers, all five! Yes, Quenten was with them and dressed like them too. I looked in amazement as they all marched on toward the fire pit, but they did they not quite make it.

Georgio saw me sitting at the tiki bar and said, "Asterid. You came!"

Everyone else turned and looked at me. Then they started waving and saying hello. It did not end there though. Soon the yellow parkas came toward the bar and crowded around me and, all speaking at once, babbled on.

"So glad to see you," Mrs. Reiner said.

"Baby Emma got a tiny raincoat, too, isn't it cute?" Miranda exclaimed.

The twins just giggled and said together, "Hi. Did you get your gift yet?"

Must be a twin thing, I figured. Before I could even answer any of them, over came Jonas and, yes, he had a yellow parka in his hand! The crowd dissipated and Jonas handed me the jacket.

"Miss Asterid, here is your souvenir," he said excitedly.

There it was! A bright, yellow parka with my name on the front and the words "Skinner's Cay" on the back.

"How nice," I said as I studied it.

"Put it on," Jake blurted out with a sarcastic smile as he busied himself mixing drinks.

"I think I will, Jake," I exclaimed to humor his sarcasm and he just nodded and smile.

"Well Miss Asterid, I must go help my brothers finish preparing vegetables," and he went on his merry way toward the fire pit. Everyone else was taking their seats at their little tables and Jake was still mixing drinks and grinning.

"An odd gift for an island that seldom sees rain, don't you think?" I asked Jake.

"Well," he said, "Jonas was supposed to pass the parkas out this morning before the fishing trip in case we got a lot of rain. Good thing we didn't because he forgot. So the parkas were handed out now. Better late than never, right?"

"Right," I agreed.

Then the grin came off his face and he said with sincerity, "You see Miss, we all falter."

I got the feeling he was not referring to just the quadruplets. I could not really tell what his implications were, but I think he was referring to me, Quenten, or the both of us. I think he knew about Quenten and me, in fact I had more than a feeling about that. I had no more to say because I had only one more day left of this vacation and there really was no time for resolving problems in a relationship that really never existed. Well, maybe it existed for a couple of days but really where was it going anyway?

I looked over at the dining area and everyone was seated at a table except me, so I casually headed over there, leaving Jake with his mixology. The aroma of fish got stronger as I neared the only empty table that was left. Good for me it was on the side closest to where I was headed. The brothers were all around the fire pit, each attending to his own frying pan, including Quenten. His back was toward me and I could see pans of colorful vegetables being flipped and seasoned systematically to a crisp fry. All seemed to be enjoying the project, as far as I could see and Quenten seemed to be interacting generously with his brothers.

How nice, I thought. But that just made me feel bad for myself, bad that he was not interacting with me. It all seemed like a dream. that I was intimate with this man that no longer knew I existed.

"Asterid, Asterid," someone was calling my name and when I looked to where the voice was echoing from. I realized it was Gregory.

I said, "Yes."

He asked, "Would you like to sit at our table?"

Then Georgio added, "Yes, do not sit by yourself. Pull up a chair."

So I did, I picked up my wooden, heavier than I expected, chair, and started toward the newlyweds. Gregory and Georgio saw me struggling with the chair and jumped up to help, but they were too late. I felt someone behind me lifting it up because by that time I was dragging it behind me. I turned to see who it was and as I thought, it was Quenten.

Oh my God! I thought. I could hardly believe he was paying attention to what I was doing. I figured he was done trying to talk to me after I did not answer the door earlier.

"Let me give you a hand," he said.

I just said, "Thank you," as I was mind drooling over his robust figure and arm muscles bulging out of the short sleeves of his white polo shirt. He did not say any more, just carried the chair over to Gregory and Georgio's table where they made room for it. Then to my surprise again, he turned and went back to the fire pit to resume cooking.

That was interesting enough, I thought. I was flustered thinking that we still have a chance and that his actions seemed contrite. I sat down at the table with the newlyweds and Georgio poured me some sangria into the glass that Gregory held.

"Here you go," he said as he handed it to me.

I took the glass and said, "Cheers. Here's to your honeymoon, hope you are having a wonderful time!"

"Thank you," they said together and we all drank. The other guests were all drinking sangria and engaging in their own conversations. Then came the platters. Each of the quads took a table and brought us each a platter of food. Jonas came over to our table with ocean blue colored dishes shaped like fish. He placed one in front of each of us and on them was a colorful display of fried fish and fried vegetables that, in combination, promoted a generous, not too fishy aroma.

Then he explained, "Here we have a trio of fried fish: ahi tuna, blue fish, and mahi mahi. Also plantains, red, green, and yellow peppers with onions, and last but not least fried potatoes or as you say 'french fries'." Then he said with a smile, "Enjoy please," and went back over to Quenten who was now setting up some equipment on a small platform in the far corner of the tent.

"I think they are having karaoke tonight." Gregory said, "Yes it looks that way."

Georgio agreed.

I added, "Yes I think so too. Do you two sing?"

"Yes," they chorused as we all started in on our meal.

The fish was so flavorful and the vegetables were crisp as a new day at sunrise.

"It's so good," I said, the boys agreed.

We continued eating the feast and I noticed the brothers making dishes of food for themselves. Then they all walked over to the tiki bar where Jake was waiting patiently for his dish also. Quenten was carrying two platters and handed one to Jake. Then the six of them sat and began eating. Everyone was enjoying the meal and all was quiet, only the clinking of silverware touching the dishes could be heard. A while later and I could no longer consume another bite. Gregory and Georgio had wiped their dishes clean and there was mine, still looking full of food.

I noticed them looking at my dish so I said, "I had a big lunch," and they smiled.

I really did have a big lunch. That burger that Rupert made me was gigantic and I did try a bite of everything on my dish. I just could not finish it. I realized that the newlyweds were more interested in when the karaoke was to begin because they started talking about what songs they would sing.

"Let's go see what songs they have," said Georgio.

Gregory obliged and then asked me, "Do you want to come, Asterid?"

"No I have not sung in a long time," I said. "But thanks."

I would not dare to look over at the tiki bar! As it turned out, I did not have to. Suddenly, I felt a hand on my shoulder, it felt warm and friendly. As I looked up I realized it was Quenten.

"May I sit?" he asked.

Shaking in my chair, I said, "Yes."

He sat and looked into my eyes with his glistening green orbs and said, "I want to apologize."

"For what?" I quickly asked. Meanwhile, I was thinking, *for attacking me when I was snooping around? For leaving me hanging last night and not calling? Or for not being truthful about being a mad scientist? Sounds crazy*, I thought. I had all these ideas scrambling around in my head.

He went on, "I came by your place today because I needed to tell you that I am sorry for everything. For being rude to you, for not explaining things to you which… there is a lot to explain, and for not showing up last night. That was so terrible of me! And…"

I then interrupted him and said, "Quenten, you do not owe me an explanation. I think we both got caught up in the excitement of being with each other and now it is over."

I could not believe I was saying these things, but I had to. I had to keep my pride because I knew in reality I would be leaving in a couple of days, probably never to see him again. That did hurt, but I was not going to let him know that.

"No, I cannot accept that, Asterid. I love you, please do not let it be over!" He had tears in his eyes and he grabbed my hands.

I wanted to cry with him but I fought back the tears as I held his hands. By now everyone was looking at us, including the brothers. Then Jonas and Sebastian came bustling over.

Sebastian announced, "Karaoke time, who wants to sing?"

Gregory and Georgio were still on the platform. They raised their hands and said, "We do."

Jonas and Sebastian handed them cordless microphones and went on the stage to show them how to pick their song. I could not help wondering how Jonas and Sebastian were going to read the songs and type them in the machine, so I kept looking.

"It's like a juke box," Quenten said. Then he added, "The guests just punch in the digits that coincide with the song they choose. My brothers do not have to do it." I looked at him with surprise and then he continued, "I know that was what you were wondering."

He was right so I said nothing. The music started and the newlyweds started singing "Sugar Sugar" by the Archies. I loved that song. The twins, the doctor and his wife got up to dance and the tent became quite loud again with the attention off Quenten and me. Thank God!

"Asterid, I need to talk to you in private. Please let me have the chance," Quenten begged, still holding my hands. He did not seem to care who saw either, he was quite sure of what he was doing which surprised me immensely.

"Okay, but this is not the time nor place Quenten," I reminded him.

"Then when?" he asked desperately. Before I could answer him, he looked again into my eyes and said, "You are beautiful and I love you."

Well, that did it, I could not resist his tenderness along with his eagerness. My heart was pounding. I yearned for him so. "Let's go," I said.

"Where?"

"To my place." I took him by the hand and he followed me right to his Jeep without drawing the attention of anyone. I jumped in his side and scooted over before he had a chance to lift me. He laughed, got in, and started the engine. The music and singing was so loud, no one even heard us leave. There we were driving toward my chalet and I became excited being with him once again, though I wondered what he had to talk to me about. We reached the chalet and he got out and ran to get me on my side of the vehicle. I fell into his arms gracefully and willingly. I wanted to make love right there and then, but I did not want to distract him from what he needed to talk to me about.

I said, "Shall we go inside?"

He nodded and carried me down the dock to my door. He continued carrying me all the way inside and placed me on the sofa. We laughed and he sat down next to me.

"Would you like some coffee or a drink?" I asked him.

"No thank you," he said.

"Neither do I," I said, "I am so full of food and drink, it will take me a week to digest."

But he seemed to be far away in his mind, as if he did not hear a word I said. He was in a daze so I took off my yellow parka that I still had on. *No wonder I was hot*! I thought.

I proceeded to the bedroom to hang it up and I heard Quenten say, "Come, sit please, Asterid," so I ran back into the sitting area and sat right next to him. "I do not know where to begin so I will just start from the beginning. I was born in a town in Pennsylvania to a wonderful, loving mother, Lillyann, and a crazy scientist father, Dr. Quenten King, Sr. I had a great childhood in spite of my father's craziness. My mother and I were always together. She read to me, took me to the park, let me have sleepovers with the kids from school, and just your normal everyday life things. My father was never home except for vacation time when he would bring us here to the island which he purchased years earlier at a cheap price. He always said we would live here for good one day and have fun all of the time and I believed him. But his intentions went much deeper than that. My father was obsessed with behavioral scientists most of his life. His God was Skinner."

My knees started shaking as Quenten continued with his story. That is just what is sounded like, a story. I could not believe what I was hearing. I started thinking, *I was right! This is a crazy island!*

Quenten saw me shaking and probably noticed the bewildered expression on my face and said calmly, "I'm not finished. Should I continue?" But he did not even wait for my response, he just continued. "As I was saying, his God was Skinner and his Bible was, 'Walden Two'. My father even traveled to Harvard University to study under Skinner for a while, but that was not enough. I sat listening and managed to keep my composure as Quenten went on. "My father thought he was a better scientist than Skinner and where Skinner's composition advocates the perfect community, my father was going to actually build and live in the perfect community!" He paused. "Am I losing you, Asterid?" he asked.

"No, not at all," I said. "Burrhus Frederic Skinner, author of 'Walden Two' which proceeded Thoreau's 'Walden' in which Thoreau actually lived as one with nature for quite some time and kept a journal of his adventures.I got it," I said, still in disbelief of what I was hearing.

Quenten nodded and said, "Okay, then I will continue. He even wanted to try little experiments with me and my mother absolutely forbade him. He was fascinated with Skinner's box or the behavioral conditioning known as operant conditioning. I remember my mother and father fighting about it a lot. She would say, 'Go to work and do your experiments, do not bring them home.' He did what she said, but I always felt like he hated me and blamed me for that.

"When I was nine, my father and mother were getting along extremely well. He spent more time at home and I figured he realized the science thing was less important than his family. At least that's what I thought. My mother was approaching forty and he fifty and he kept telling her he wanted another baby. I remember my mother laughing and saying, 'Oh Quenten, we're too old!' I was just a boy, but even I thought it was strange and could not help but to think that I was a disappointment. I was not the son he wanted and he wanted to try again and do it right this time! My father kept hounding my mother and I do not know if she was tired of listening to him or love struck by his new found charisma, but she agreed to have another. She did not have an easy time becoming pregnant and they were frustrated and tired of trying. Just as they were about to give up, my mother became pregnant. Father was so happy, he was even extra nice to me so I did not mind and when the doctor told us I could have not one but maybe four brothers or sisters, I became more excited and so did my parents. But the excitement would be short lived, at least for me anyway. My mother gave birth to four baby boys: Jonas, Lucas, Rupert and Sebastian. Yes, all beautiful and healthy but my mother was not healthy. She had lost a lot of blood and her health deteriorated rapidly during the days following the childbirth. The doctors said there was nothing they could do and she was dying."

At this point I had tears in my eyes and I said to Quenten, "Do you want to stop, Quenten?" I just wanted to rescue both of us from the sadness which filled the room.

He looked at me in such an appreciative way and said, "No, I need to finish."

"Alright," I said, "take your time."

"I went to visit my mother on the day she died and she kissed me and said, 'I love you little man, please always take care of your brothers.'

"I sobbed and sobbed and then I said to her, 'Don't worry, Mom, I always will.' She smiled and then she was gone. Just like that. I could not help but think the only person in the world that I had was gone. It was strange that I thought, that seeing I had a father and four brothers but I was right! A few weeks later, father brought the babies home from the hospital and informed me that I would be going away to boarding school.

"'I cannot go, Dad, I promised Mom I would take care of the babies!' is what I said to him and he did not reply, he just sent me away to Hawaii.

"There I was in a strange place, a beautiful place indeed, but just the same strange to me. I liked the boarding school but I missed my mother and the baby brothers I never got to know, let alone protect. Protect from that insane man I called 'Dad'. The same man that never called, wrote, or came to see me for the next twenty years! I adjusted well to my school, my teachers, and friends over time but I never forgot my home and my mom. I just concentrated on my studies and enjoyed the beautiful island and ocean. I went on to college and got my own apartment and my life was okay. Home seemed like a dream that I once had, a wonderful dream I would never forget. But as it turned out I would not have a chance to forget. On a sunny day in June, I was sitting at my kitchen table and I heard a knock at my door, which was a little strange because I did not have many visitors ever. I was kind of a loner."

That's a surprise, I thought and then I cleared my throat.

"Do you need a break?" Quenten asked.

"No go on, Quenten," I said. "I want to hear this." It was like listening to a story of fiction. It was hard to believe it was true, but I endured and so did he.

"I opened the door and it was a man who said he was my father's attorney and that my father had a massive heart attack and had died on the island."

What island? I wondered.

"It had been so long, I had almost forgotten about the island my father owned. Then he handed me the will, a letter from my father to me, and a box filled with notebooks of my father's work.

"The attorney advised me, 'Everything you need is here, your father instructed me to bring everything to you if he should die,' Then he left, just turned and disappeared like he was a flower delivery guy or something. Dad's will said that all his assets were left to me: the island, the money, and my brothers! The letter was his idea of an apology I guess and a request for me to continue his work, which I assumed was in the stack of notebooks in the box he had sent.

"I stayed home from work the next day to begin trying to figure out what I needed to do. The attorney had already had my father cremated and there was to be no funeral, those were my father's wishes. My main concern was for my brothers. Where were they? Who were they? How were they doing? What were they doing? I knew I would find the dreaded answers in his notebooks, so I started reading them. It took all day, but I finally finished them and all I could think was, *I hate that man*! He really went too far."

I could not help but interrupt Quenten so I asked him, "What did he do? What was in the notebooks?"

Quenten continued, "After he sent me away, he quit his job at the Pennsylvania Medical Center and decided he was going to raise the babies on his own, his way! He had the island in mind the whole time. He decided to condition each of the boys to do a certain task so that they could move to the island he named 'Skinner's Cay', after his idol. 'It will be better than Skinner's Walden Two!' he wrote.

"Our house in Pennsylvania was like a mansion. It had numerous large rooms. The rooms were each the size of regular house. So, he began his mission.

"He wanted to turn Skinner's Cay into a community of perfection. He wanted it to have activities, music, art, dancing, and good food. He wanted nobody to want for anything. He wanted it to be perfect so he started conditioning the quadruplets at an early age. He made one of the large rooms into a nursery with four cribs, a changing table, bath net, and all the amenities babies need. He fed, changed, and took care of them as a father should, at least for the first few years. At three years of age, when they could walk and talk, he designed a big play room to simulate the island. There was a kiddie pool in one corner and toy drums, a toy piano and a toy banjo in another corner. The third corner had a toy kitchen set, table, chairs, a play stove, a toy shopping cart with plastic food, and even a toy fridge. The fourth corner hosted a plastic easel, an art table with coloring books, crayons, paints, and sketching paper. He taught the boys to swim in the little pool, he played supermarket and pretend cooking with them. He participated in their music concerts with their toy instruments and they all colored together and drew pictures.

"Father played with them every day for two years. Eventually, the boys seemed to migrate to the corner that most interested them. Lucas loved the pool, Rupert loved to pretend to cook, Sebastian banged away on the drums and piano, and Jonas would draw and paint all day. Father decided it was time for them to have their own bedrooms. Each equipped with a bed, a dresser, and a TV with a VCR. He decided that Lucas was going to be the swimmer, so he could be the lifeguard of the community and teach others to swim and do water activities. He had an almost Olympic size swimming pool put in Lucas' room, heated of course. 'For comfort,' he wrote but that was ironic, my brother's life seemed anything but comfortable. Lucas loved swimming in the big pool, but that was not enough. He bought him VHS tapes and made him watch hours of tapes on swimming and swimming techniques. The rest of the time was spent in the pool. If he got tired and wanted to get out, he would not let him and even turned the heater off until he complied."

Quenten kept speaking, fighting back the tears and wiping the ones he could not fight. I was sobbing quietly for my heart went out to not only Lucas but to Quenten as well. Though in distress, he plowed on through and went on to Sebastian.

"Sebastian, my father decided, would be the musician. His room looked like the philharmonic. He had a piano, a trumpet, a guitar, drums, and every kind of horn you could imagine. He learned to play each instrument by watching instructional tapes that showed where to put each finger to play each song. After ten hours a day of that, he mastered most instruments quickly. He would play the guitar until his fingers bled. If he complained, he would not even be allowed to put band-aids on his fingers, he would have to play with them raw from the wear of the guitar strings.

"Rupert would be the chef, father decided. His room consisted of a stove, a fridge, a sink along with all the cooking utensils, condiments, and food one could imagine! Of course, I must not forget a fire extinguisher. After all, he was cooking gourmet food at the age of five."

Quenten was becoming agitated and made a fist with both hands as he went on but he did go on. "Again, he was made to watch tapes about food, how to prepare it, how to cut it, and how to serve it. Father would have him prepare a big feast for the entire family every night. If it was not to Father's or the other boys' satisfaction, he would have to prepare the same meal over and over again until it was. When he did not comply, or even complained, he would not be allowed to eat the food he so diligently prepared all day and he would go to bed hungry!

"Last but not least was Jonas. Jonas was supposed to be the artist, in his room were easels, canvasses, paints, drawing pencils, markers, paper, frames, and anything one would need in an art studio. He too watched tapes on painting, drawing, and art galleries. He seemed to enjoy it and never got tired of painting and drawing. Father never had a problem with him wanting to paint. Jonas just was terrible at it. Father got so mad he even made him paint the entire house at five years old and told him he could not stop until he was finished. He did not even mind that. He stayed on the ladder for three days and almost died of dehydration and exhaustion. Of course my nutcase father did not even take him to the hospital. He gave him an IV and put him in bed for a week until he regained his strength.

"Father wrote that Jonas was his variable and it would be a challenge to condition him. He kind of gave up on him, but he noticed Jonas would go to each of his brother's rooms each day bringing them a drink or seeing if they needed anything. So he decided that Jonas would be a good host on his island. Father called him 'my useless meet and greet'. What a cold-hearted man! My brothers' lives continued this way for the next five years, only being allowed to rest from their activities to eat, bathe, and sleep."

Quenten stopped talking for a moment, I did not know if he was reflecting or taking a breather, but I was thirsty and said, "I am getting a bottle of water, would you like one?"

"Yes please," he said. His face was flushed and his eyes looked tired but that did not stop him from going on with the story, "So, by the age of ten, Father started to worry about the boys not attending school or ever seeing other people. He figured he had better flee from Pennsylvania while they were still under the radar. So he packed the boys up and headed here. Meanwhile, Father's health started to fail. He developed a heart condition which he treated himself, but he tired easily and lost his strength. He and the boys lived on the island in a small hut he had built when he took me and my mother there years earlier. The boys continued, 'doing what they do'. Jonas made sure everyone had what they needed, Lucas swam in the big ocean, Sebastian entertained them all with his instruments and Rupert cooked, mostly fish. vegetables and plants that were on the island. Father still had his dream of the perfect community. He and the boys started building chalets for the community Father told them they would have. They used wood from the palm trees and the tools that Father brought with him."

I got the bottles of water from the fridge, still listening, and handed one to Quenten. We both drank them like fish in the desert and then as I sat next to him he went on.

"With Father being sick and the boys, or should I say men by now, not knowing much about building, the project became endless. That's when he must have had the heart attack because the notes in his book stopped. It took me a while to absorb it all. I cannot say I was surprised, but I was so sad for my brothers and myself. We never even knew each other and I promised my mom I would take care of them."

What a lie. I thought. "Quenten, your father sent you away. There was nothing you could have done and your mother knows that!" I told him.

"Do you believe that, Asterid?" he asked me.

"Absolutely," I said. "I know my mother is always here with me in spirit, even now."

"I'm sorry for your loss, Asterid," he then said to me, putting his head on my shoulder.

I just held him and said, "I know, as I am sorry for yours." Then I asked, "So, when did you come here, Quenten?"

He went on with his story.

"I came the the next day. The attorney never said how my brothers were or if they even asked for me, but I came anyway. When I arrived, they were all disoriented. Jonas was walking around in circles with a tray of drinks in his hands and talking to himself. Sebastian was pounding on the piano and not playing anything that remotely resembled a tune. Rupert was cooking on a hibachi and burning what looked like was once fish and Lucas was swimming in a circle like a shark circling a surfer.

"I did not know where to begin, but that was not difficult. They all spotted me at the same time and stopped what they were doing immediately. Then they charged at me like wild bulls but they did not attack. They all hugged me and would not let go. Then they kept saying, 'Our brother! Our brother!' I did not know what to say or do. I just cried and said, 'I'm sorry, I'm sorry.'

"It was in that moment I decided that the promise I made to my mother twenty years earlier would be kept. But it turns out that was easier said than done. Though they were my brothers, I really did not even know them, nor did they know me. They could not read, reason, or really relate to me or anyone else. We started by finishing building the chalets. One by one we, or should I say I, built them. My brothers had good intentions but for them the swimming, cooking, and music took precedent over trying to build a resort fit for guests and we needed guests. My brothers had never interacted with other people and I was not going to isolate them any longer. In between building the chalets, I started to teach them how to read and write, but that was like pulling teeth. It still is difficult. But that's what you heard when you came along."

"Quenten, I am so sorry I was snooping. I just wanted to see you. I was so impatient that I did not want to wait until you came back that night. I never meant to do that, I just got excited. When I realized the meeting was outside, I thought I could get a glimpse of you and be on my way. I was not prying but I know it did not look that way."

"Oh Asterid, I was not mad at you. I was mad at me and was ashamed for not being honest with you. Can you forgive me for not showing up last night?"

"Of course I forgive you. I feel so bad that I was angry at all. But Quenten, don't you think your brothers would be better off with a good psychiatrist, instead of you trying to 'un-condition' them yourself? That is what you are trying to do, am I wrong?" I asked him.

"No, you are not wrong and I am a good psychiatrist," he said.

"No, you are an accountant," I answered deliberately.

"No, I am just good at numbers. I am a psychiatrist and had my own practice in Hawaii. Well, Jake and I had our own practice," he insisted.

I looked at him amazed. All I could think to say is, "I knew Jake was not a real bartender."

We both laughed and it cut the tension a bit.

Then he added, "Jake was getting ready to retire and had lost his wife years ago when they were very young. She became ill and passed, they never had children. He said that I was the only family he had. When I left, he sold our practice and joined me here. 'A friend in need is a friend indeed,' he said as he got off the water taxi the day he arrived. He has been here for me and my brothers ever since."

I replied, "You are lucky to have Jake and your brothers are lucky to have you."

"I finished the resort, with Jake's help, in about two years. A year later, in 1993, we opened for business. I am glad that I finally got to be with my brothers, but I still feel lonely. They do not know me like they know each other. They have always been together and survived my father together. I cannot relate to them like they do to each other and sometimes I feel like I am trapped here. Don't get me wrong, I love the island and I love that people enjoy it here. I cannot explain how I feel."

"Well, I can tell you that I am tired and you look tired too," I said to Quenten.. I was changing the subject because I was exhausted and a little in shock from all I had heard. When I was hypothesizing about the island being like Walden Two, I was almost positive I was being crazy. But it turned out I was not so crazy after all!

Quenten looked at me and held my face in his hands and then said, "I love you."

I said, "I love you too."

I did love him and the fact that he told me all his dark secrets proved that he really did love me. I leaned back in his arms and we sat quiet on the sofa. I felt like I was in an alternate reality and that maybe this was not really happening. I wanted his love and I wanted his desire, but did I really want his truths. I was worn, distraught and tired so I just laid in his arms...I was tired.

Day 6 - May 6th, 2005

I woke up on the sofa. I knew I was still in the sitting room because I was staring at the kitchenette as I lay with my head on the pillow.

Pillow! I thought, *How did I wind up lying down with a pillow?* Then I saw a tall figure walk in from the deck. It was Quenten, still in his clothes from the evening before. So was I, for that matter, except my shoes.

"Morning," he said. "I got you a pillow and took off your shoes last night. You had fallen sound asleep, I hope you don't mind."

"No," I said, "Where did you sleep?"

"I slept on the floor. I was so tired, I could have slept on nails," he said. We both smiled. "I made coffee," he said as he poured two cups.

I need that so much, I thought. I needed to wake my tired mind that was saddened by all I had learned to be true. At the same time, the thought of Quenten being here in my chalet excited me! His presence always excited me and made me want him more! Quenten came over to the sofa as I sat up to greet him. He handed me my coffee and then went over to the fridge, removed some creamers from the shelf, and took sugar packets from a container on the counter, and brought them over to me.

"Oh, you need a spoon for your ten packs of sugar!"

"Don't be funny," I said. "You know I do."

He went over to a drawer, took out the spoon, and came back over to the sofa with his coffee cup in hand also. We sat on the sofa, he drinking his coffee and I mixing mine. I finally caught up to him, took my first sip, and thought, *Ah, life is good again.*

He enjoyed watching me I think because he smiled and said, "There you are. Good, right?"

I laughed at his statement and agreed, nodding my head. I probably looked a mess but if I did, he did not see it. I knew that because he gazed at me and said, "You are so beautiful."

"As are you," I said. He started to blush and I said, "Oh, I do not mean to make you feel uncomfortable, Quenten."

"You could never make me feel uncomfortable, you are the best thing that ever happened to me. I want you to marry me." The words just flowed out of him as if he had rehearsed the scene over and over, or maybe because they came from his heart.

My heart was not as fluent because I was not prepared for that question. In fact I was surprised. I mean, I thought about it over and over. About being his wife and swinging in his hammock forever, him smiling at me with those gorgeous green eyes, holding me in those arms of steel, the happily ever after story!

I must have been deep in thought because all of a sudden I heard Quenten saying, "Asterid, did you hear me?"

I looked at him and said, "Yes," with hesitation,. Yes I heard you but…"

He interrupted me by saying, "But what, Asterid? I thought you loved me. Was I mistaken?"

"No." I could not think of the right words to say, so I just said it. "I need time to think, Quenten. This has all come too fast. I do love you, but I have my Dad back home who has only me. I have my patients and…"

Then he grabbed my arms and said, "Do not worry! I will send for your Dad today and you can refer your patients to someone you trust. You do have colleagues, don't you?"

"I do, but that is my career."

Then he laughed and said, "Oh, the money? I have more money than

I could ever spend in a lifetime. You and your father will never have to worry. I will take care of you both always."

He seemed to have it all figured out, but I did not!

"Quenten, it is not that easy," I said to him.

He then let go of my arms and stared into my eyes. He looked heartbroken and bit angry at the same time, "Love should be easy. It is for me, so I guess I will take all you've said as a no!"

He then turned and walked out the door and never turned back. I remained on the sofa in tears as I heard him start up his Jeep and speed away down the road.

"What have I done?" I asked myself out loud. I have probably lost the only man that I have ever loved and probably was my soul mate. I did not want to end our relationship, I just wanted more time to prepare, to tell my dad, and to decide if I could live here forever. He did not understand where I was coming from. *Maybe it was for the best*, I thought.

Beep, beep, beep.

There it was, the lovely sound of the intercom. I thought sarcastically. "Hello," I said.

"Hello, Miss." It was Tevin of course.

"Yes, Tevin," I said, not happily. But he paid no mind to my abruptness.

"Will you be attending the send-off Saturday all-day buffet and beach games today? I will pick you up. They begin in an hour or so."

"No, I am going to start packing. What time is my departure in the morning?"

Tevin said, "8:00 a.m., Miss. But you can come to the beach party for a little while and I can take you back to your chalet at whatever time you wish."

He was being so kind but I was not in the mood to go anywhere so I said nicely this time, "No thanks, just the same Tevin. I will call you if I decide otherwise."

"Very well Miss, should I bring you lunch at least?"

"I am not hungry, but I will let you know if I need something to eat," I said to him.

"Okay. Bye," is all I heard and he was off the intercom.

I stared shaking and crying and thinking. *What have I done?* Not to Tevin, to Quenten. He had been through so much in his life and overcome so many obstacles. *Would I be his biggest obstacle of all?* I wondered.

I went to the bedroom and looked in the vanity mirror to see a red eyed, wild haired and smudged makeuped me! *Quenten's disappointment!* I thought. I was disappointed too, with myself, with him, and with the entire world. They say the most important decisions we make are the ones that we have to live with for the rest of our lives. But I really did not make the decision. He did, he walked out on me. Yes, he probably thought he had a good reason, but we could have tried to sort things out.

No matter, I guessed, *I was leaving and he was staying and that was that. Maybe there would be no more said.* I reluctantly started to gather my suitcases and one at the time, opened them on the floor of the bedroom. Out of character, I threw clothes from the drawers into each suitcase with no regard to organization. I had one goal only to empty the drawers, fill the luggage. With that in mind only, I could stay focused. I emptied the wardrobe, the bathroom shelves that contained my toiletries, the vanity top with my hair supplies, and anything else that was mine. I kept tearing up, hating myself and hating Quenten, all the time I was packing. I was like a wild woman throwing things into the luggage wherever they would fit, thinking, *why did I bring so many clothes? I did not need half of them.* I wondered what time it was, so I stopped what I was doing and went out to the kitchen drawer to retrieve my phone. *The only thing it was good for on this island was the time,* I figured. I turned it on and it was 2:00 p.m. *Great,* I thought sarcastically, *only another eighteen hours before my departure.* I needed to calm down and be rational, after all this was my doing too. I wanted that man since the first time I laid eyes on him. I think I wanted him the minute I saw him in the painting on the wall of the dining hut.

I decided I needed fresh air, so I went out to the deck and sat in the lounger for what would be my last glimpse of my ocean view. For a while it was beautiful. The sun was hot and bright, the waves were in sync with the ocean that consumed them so willingly, and the birds that flew above them simultaneously. *Why can't people be in harmony like that? Because we think too much, that's why*, I thought, answering my own question.

I sat there and put my head back to absorb the rays of the shining sun, it was so warm and satisfying. It lead me to good thoughts finally, thoughts of my first few days with Quenten. I pictured his smile when we were on the boat and I pictured us in the water splashing each other like little kids playing in a swimming pool. It was if there was no one else in the world but the two of us. I pictured his sexiness when we made love and my willingness to oblige however I could, to let go of all of my inhibitions. Then I thought, *maybe he will come back even if it was to say goodbye, I would at least have that.*

I sat there daydreaming for what seemed like a moment but was actually hours. I felt my face burning and realized I had been in the sun for a long time. The waves and the wind were picking up too. I decided to go in and once again retrieve my phone which had transformed to be my only track of time. It was 5:00 p.m. and I still had the rest of the evening to occupy, hopefully in good form. I decided to shower, since I had not even washed my face or brushed my teeth yet.

I started for the bathroom but was interrupted by a knock at the door. I just stopped in my steps. I froze, thinking, *it's Quenten! He's come back!* Then, disheartened I heard the sound of a voice saying, "Miss? Are you there?"

"No," I said and laughed to myself. *No time like the present for a little humor*, I thought and headed toward the door. I opened the door and there was Tevin, smiling as usual and looking much tidier than the night before. He didn't smell like fish either.

"Hello Tevin," I said, still giggling about saying "no" when he had asked if I was here.

"Oh, sorry to bother you but I have some dinner for you," he explained handing me a brown bag that smelled good and made me think of food for the first time all day. "You did not make it to the main beach, so I thought you might be hungry by now."

"Well. You were right. Thank you Tevin, have a good night," I said to him. I proceeded to shut the door and he continued to speak.

"Just one more thing, Miss. I will pick you up at 7:30 a.m. so you will make your water taxi on time. Is that fine?" he asked.

"Yes, it is. Thank you," I said.

Then he nodded, turned around, and left. I waited until I was sure he had nothing more to say and then shut the door, holding the brown bagged dinner in my hand. I went over to the kitchen table, put it down, and began to open it when I started to feel sick to my stomach. I think I was too stressed out from everything to be hungry and, though it smelled so good, I could not even bring myself to open the bag and see what meal Tevin had gathered. So I just left the bag there and went on to the bathroom.

I got my clothes off and jumped into the shower that was long overdue. I lathered up with my complimentary toiletries, considering I had already packed all of mine, and, smelling the strawberry body wash, continued to wash aimlessly. The warmth of the shower comforted me. *My first comfort of the day*, I thought. I stood there scrubbing and not thinking too much. Maybe I could wash away all the sadness I had if I stayed here long enough, I figured. My mouth was so dry, I took some of the mouthwash provided on the shower shelf, rinsed, and spit. I kept rinsing until my mouth no longer felt gross like the rest of me.

Maybe if I stayed here all night, morning would come sooner, I thought. *No, that probably would not work. I would have a glass of wine and fall asleep, so the night would go by and I would not think.* With that plan in mind, I quickly turned the water off, grabbed a towel off the rack, and wrapped up in it. I leaned sideways to ring the excess water from my hair and then stepped out of the tub without even drying up. I took my complimentary white bath robe, dropped the towel, and put it on. I did feel refreshed, but so thirsty. I had not had anything to drink since Quenten made the coffee this morning I realized, so I went to the kitchen, took a bottle of rose off of the counter. I opened it, took a glass from the cupboard, and poured. I did not pour too much. I was not celebrating, just quenching my thirst and I wanted to be up in time to leave. That was the plan.

I had to stay on track with these kinds of thoughtsor I would just get into a rut again with my heart and thoughts of Quenten.

I took my glass of wine out to the deck. I stood at the edge, watching the sun descend. *It too was getting ready for bed*, I thought, *after all it had done its job for the day. The ocean too,* I thought. It was calm and quiet, probably settling down to gear up for a new day, another adventure, always the same yet somehow different. I sipped my wine and rested my mind as I watched nature resting, wishing I could rest too. Soon I grew tired and could no longer stand there, so I ventured back inside where I placed my half full glass on the counter and headed toward the bedroom to take refuge in my canopy. Well, at least it was mine for one more night. I got in and pulled the sheets up to try to get comfortable as I lay staring at the covering that separated me from the ceiling and the sky. *Another obstacle,* I thought. *They just seem to be all around me.* I closed my eyes to alleviate the heaviness of my lids, and heavy they were, like the entire day was resting on then. I just wanted to sleep.

Day 7 – May 7th, 2005

Beep, beep, beep.

I opened my eyes to that familiar call, the call of the intercom for the last time. I got out of bed and went into the sitting room to answer it.

"Hello Tevin," I said, somehow hoping in the back of my mind that it would be Quenten. But it wasn't.

"Hello Miss, are you awake?"

"Yes," I said, "I am speaking to you."

He laughed and continued with, "I will be there in half an hour to pick you up. This is your big day, yes?"

"Yes," I said.

"I will see you then," he added and he was gone or at least his voice was gone. I went straight to the coffee pot, brewed a cup, and poured it quickly. I needed to be ready by the time Tevin arrived. So, to the fridge then the counter, I poured my coffee, mixed it, and drank it all in a matter of minutes. Then I went back to the bedroom to close my five pieces of luggage when I realized I did not leave an outfit out to where for departure. *Well I can't go naked.* So I picked out the first thing I could find, a long, black gauze dress that buttoned all the way down in the front. It was plain, it was easy. *Now I just needed to find undies*, I thought and it was then I spotted black panties and a black bra on the top of the clothes in another suitcase. Sandals were easy. My black flip-flops were in the shoe suitcase with the rest of the shoes that I managed to keep together. I was dressed in no time, my suitcases were zipped, and I was ready for Tevin's arrival. I was happy with that at least. I would soon be on way home to see my Dad and get on with my life, whatever life that would be. I was not sure, but at least I still knew that I did have some kind of a life.

I brushed my hair as I waited for Tevin patiently. The wait was not long because I soon heard the knock at the door, though he was a bit early. Once again, my thoughts of grandeur took over and I imagined it was Quenten. *What if it is,* I thought, *and he wanted to apologize and start over.* Then I stopped, because as I opened the door and saw it was Tevin!

"Come in, Tevin," I said.

"Good morning, Miss," he had a dolly for my luggage, he rolled it into my bedroom wearing his khaki shorts and a khaki colored tee and black sneakers.

He did not just enter the bedroom until I said, "Go right, Tevin."

He was so polite, everyone was here. I cannot say one bad thing about any of them, I thought. Tevin loaded all five pieces in the dolly and started towards the door. I followed him closely, for he seemed to be on a mission. I could not blame him, he worked hard all week. He probably will get the rest of the day off after he gets me off on my way. We reached Tevin's buggy and he loaded my luggage into the back of the vehicle.

"Can I help?" I offered.

"Oh no thank you, Miss. Just climb in, I will be finished in a few minutes," he said.

So I got in, making sure I had my handbag that I remembered to grab off the sofa at the last minute. My plane tickets and passport were in it and I needed those if I was going to make it home. Tevin finished and joined me in the front seat. He started the buggy and off we went. We drove by the main beach area where there was not a soul to be found, let alone a bird or an iguana.

"Is everyone sleeping?" I asked Tevin.

"Yes," he said, "the other guests are leaving later, your flight is the earliest. The brothers all said their goodbyes yesterday at the send-off party. I'm sorry you missed it."

"Oh no worries," I said. Thinking, *I did miss it. So why would I expect a sendoff today? Besides Tevin was my host, driver, and sendoff person today and that was good enough for me.* We soon passed the entire island and arrived at the dock. There was the water taxi and the captain waving at us.

"Hello again," I said.

He took his hat off and said, "We meet again, Miss. Hope your vacation was enjoyable."

"It was," I assured him, or at least I hoped he was assured. After all, how could anyone not enjoy this place, at least any normal person. Tevin walked over to captain, shook his hand, and they both started to load my luggage onto the boat.

When they were finished, Tevin came over, teary eyed and long faced, and said, "Goodbye, Miss, it was a pleasure."

"Oh," I said, "it was my pleasure Tevin. Thank you for everything."

Then he looked startled and said, "Wait, I almost forgot. Mr. Quenten left something in the buggy for me to give you."

He ran to the buggy and took out a big square package wrapped in brown paper, taped on the sides. "He said he hopes you find the right place for it."

"What is it?" I asked.

"Oh I do not know, I am just the delivery man," he said with a smile.

I took the package, said thank you, and turned to where the captain was waiting for me at the entrance of the water taxi. He looked at me carrying the gift and said, "All set, Miss?"

"Yes," I sadly said.

He could tell I was upset about the package, though I did not know what it was. If I had to guess, I would say it was a painting, probably the one that was going to be of me in the hammock. I took a seat in the back and captain went up to the front, took the wheel, and off we went.

I could no longer endure wondering what was in the package so first I made sure the captain was busy manning his vessel before I quietly removed the tape from the paper and opened it up. It was a painting and it was the one I thought it would be, well sort of. There was the beautiful beach, the blue sky, the white sand, and the hammock, which hung from the two tall palm trees just as it looked in Quenten's yard. Then there I was, lying in the hammock wearing my purple romper and there was Quenten lying next to me, with white shorts, bare chested, holding me in his arms, both smiling, both in love. My tears were intervened by a loud call from captain from the front of the boat. "You'll be home in no time!" he yelled.

May 5th, 2011 – 12:00 pm.

I had just finished reading the last line and I heard my husband from the bottom of the stairs calling, "Asterid, I'm back. I have the boys and your father with me, ready to go swimming." I did not answer him right away so he came running up to the bedroom. "You're still reading that?" he asked.

I said, "Yes, Quenten. I seemed to have forgotten to finish the last page." Yes, I did say Quenten! Earlier, when he was referring to that crazy man on that crazy island, he was speaking of himself. It was his sarcastic way of joking and my sarcastic way of agreeing.

"I'll wait here while you finish," he said.

So I started writing as I continued to look at the painting and I continued to hear Tevin's voice in my head saying "Mr. Quenten said he hopes you find the right place for it," and the captain yelling, "soon you will be home".

I started to think, *I am home and I know the right place for this painting.* "Turn the boat around, Captain."

"What?" he said.

"Turn the boat around," I said, "I am home!" He seemed reluctant, so I added, "Mr. Quenten will be so upset if you do not go back!"

He then stopped the engine and walked back toward me, he looked down at the painting and said, "He certainly will," with a big smile.

He then proceeded back to his set, started the engine and headed back to Skinner's Cay. When we reached the dock, I jumped off the boat so fast I nearly landed in the water. Painting in hand and kicking off my flip flops, I ran the entire five mile stretch to Quenten's place, without stopping, thinking, or reflecting.

I knew I wanted him and where he was, I would be. Out of breath and sweating from the run, I ran to the door and started banging on it, no answer. Then I looked around and there he was, laying in the hammock. I walked over to him and he sat up with tears running down his face and the sound of uncontrollable crying.

Then he stood up and said, "What are you doing here?"

"I found the right place for the painting and for me!"

He grabbed me and held me tighter than I've ever been held before!

We sent for my father the next day. It turns out it he did not take much convincing when I told him I was marrying a rich man who owned the island and that he could build his own chalet and live there with us. He put up no argument. He said he was ready to sell his business anyway and, as far as my patients go, I referred them all to a good friend of mine Kiera, who is a great psychologist. For the inconvenience, Quenten gave them all free vouchers to visit the island whenever they wanted. It turns out they visit a little too much, so Quenten and Dad are in the process of building them their own ten room guest house. Quenten and I married on May 10th, of that same week. Jake was also a minister, so he performed the ceremony.

About a year later, I gave birth to not four, but five boys: Quenten Jr., little Rupert, little Sebastian, little Jonas, and little Lucas. We turned Quenten's painting workshop into a bedroom for the boys, with bunk beds. As for the walls, they are no longer empty. They are full of paintings, pictures, and love, with the painting of Quenten and me in the hammock right in the middle.

I would not trade my life for anything and Dad is happy here too. He bickers sometimes, mostly about Quenten's brothers. He says there is something strange about them, but I just ignore him. What am I supposed to do? I cannot tell him the whole story, after all. He does not even know who Skinner is. We have a new technique here too, contrary to Quenten's "unconditioning", I came up with "all conditioning". We all participate in each of the activities, but we do them together, in moderation of course. Today is swimming with Uncle Lucas. I have to call him that because without the prefixes "uncle" and "little" it gets very confusing around here. As for the Thursday "staff meetings," they are still going on except they're not for reading lessons. Now Quenten is giving his brothers math lessons, they are now fluent readers. "Asterid! Are you ready?" Quenten asked again.

"Yes honey, I just had to finish my journal."

"So, can I read it or not."

I looked at him, gave him a big kiss and replied, "Mmmmm. No!"

Special Thanks to:

My husband, for his support and belief in me.

My daughter who, like my mother, guides me with her love and goodness.

My Son, who has always routed for me and helped me with his brilliant computer skills during my book's composition.

My son-in-law for thinking everything I do is wonderful.

My Dad, whose hidden wisdom always surfaces when I need his advice.

My brother, who taught me that my most difficult goals could be reached with hard work and determination.

My sister, who still treats me like the princess I thought I was when we were kids.

CPSIA information can be obtained
at www.ICGtesting.com
Printed in the USA
JSHW021116071119
2318JS00001B/3